SEX & SATISFACTION 2

A collection of twenty erotic stories

Edited by Miranda Forbes

Published by Accent Press Ltd – 2009
ISBN 9781906373726

Printed and bound in the UK

Cover Design by
Red Dot Design

Contents

Contents

Lord of the Shades
by Fransiska Sherwood

I listen.

Everything's quiet. Too quiet.

Are the guards still behind me?

I wipe a streak of hair out of my face and catch my breath. But I can't stand still for long, the hounds will scent me out. At any moment I might hear their frenzied barking, or feel their foetid breath on my neck.

I shiver in my flimsy dress, intended for a cocktail party, not a mission of espionage. Why ever did I agree to go through with it? The hope of reward? Fool to think he'd have softened to me then, declared any kind of feelings.

I remember the promise in his eyes, the wicked gleam when I agreed to carry out his plan. 'Don't disappoint me,' he said, 'and I won't disappoint you.' His finger slowly traced a snaking line over my stomach, curling down towards the moist slit between my legs. Briefly he rubbed the nub of my clitoris through the slinky material of my dress. 'But first you've got to earn it.'

I trembled with fear and pleasure, anticipating one of his 'games' when I returned with the files he desired. What would he have me do? Would he dress me up? Have me wait on him? Serve me my pleasures with

1

morsels of food? Or make me beg for his favours until I cracked?

I run on until a railway tunnel opens up in the darkness in front of me. I must be on a disused line.

A mossy pungency oozes out of its mouth and I'm embraced by a cold clamminess. I hesitate, my heart beating with new fear.

But I've got to keep going. Down into the tunnel, whatever it might hold. It's the only chance they may lose my scent.

Cobbled granite chunks shift beneath my tread, twisting and throwing my ankles in their unsuitable, silver-heeled shoes.

Darkness engulfs me, and icy pearls of water drip from the ceiling and tickle my neck. Inside the tunnel it's blacker by far than the night outside. The moon's unable to penetrate these depths.

I venture further.

Slowly, silently, stealthily does it, I tell myself. Keep to the edge, close to the wall.

My feet crunch the ground, the sound magnified and echoed the length of the tunnel and back. I feel like an impostor, entering a forbidden realm, and, the deeper into the tunnel I go, the greater the feeling I'm being watched by invisible eyes.

Is there anyone here? I call softly.

There's no reply.

Perhaps they're only the eyes of toads, rats and weasels? But such creatures are the harbingers of another lord, ruler of the Underworld. Forerunners sent out to welcome the unwary.

I halt, but all I can hear is the beating of my own heart. I must get a grip on myself. It's just my terrified imagination creating fiends. Why should there be anyone down here?

Gradually my pulse starts to normalise and I gather my wits and senses about me.

For the moment I seem to have shaken off my trackers. What now? Should I wait here or go deeper into the tunnel? Or perhaps make my way back to the Old Hall, where the party would now be in full swing. Foreign delegates flirting with the hostesses, diplomats making small talk. Maybe I could slip back inside unnoticed, pretend I'd been called upon to interpret for someone in some other room. But return empty-handed with no information to pass to my lover? A man who expected service before he bestowed any favours.

Cold eventually prompts me to move on. Wearily now, joints stiffening, I continue along the wall, my fingers running over its slimy, glacial surface, tentatively feeling their way forward.

And then the wall comes to an abrupt end. And in the gap there's something softer. Something made of cloth. The moment I touch it, a big hot hand smothers my mouth, throttling my cry. My heart leaps into my throat. I'm expecting the end to be swift. But instead of crushing me, the man concealed in the darkness pulls me towards him.

'Shh!'

I sag into his arms. I can feel the pounding of his heart through his coat as my cheek rests against it. He's keyed, muscles taut, senses flexed.

Who is he? Not the Lord of Hades, after all. Or if he is, I was misled into believing him a fiend. And he can't be one of the security guards. Nor is he a tramp; he smells divine. Some rich, exotic fragrance. Sandalwood and cinnamon. Mingled with a slight hint of sweat. Has he, too, been running? Another guest from the party? But why would he be hiding down here? Why would anyone be out here, in the middle of nowhere?

Eventually he relaxes, and I feel his breath tickle my skin as it streams into my face and envelops me with its warmth. I shiver at the sensation. He fumbles with the buttons of his coat, takes his arms out of the sleeves, drapes the heavy material over my shoulders, wrapping me within its folds. I nestle against him.

'Thanks,' I whisper. He presses his fingers to my lips. Like blowing a kiss.

Shrouded in the coat we wait and listen in silence, our hearts ticking over. All stations on alert. For long minute after minute.

We hear nothing.

Nothing but each other's muffled breathing. Our hearts pounding against each other through the thin material of our clothes.

The texture of his shirt, its smooth, flowing sheen, tells me it must be silk. It tickles my nipples as they rub against him when I move. And my fingers, seeking something to hold on to, detect at his waist the satin folds of a cummerbund.

He's got to be someone from the cocktail party. Who else would be dressed like this?

'Who are you?' I whisper.

'Quiet.' His voice is low and deep, with an unmistakable foreignness to it. One of the diplomats? Certainly none of those I know.

There's something in the accent I can't pinpoint. I don't think he's Russian. Something more exotic, like Estonian, Lithuanian. Finnish, even? But somehow I imagine him to be dark. With a warm, southern temperament, more like the Greeks and Italians. But he's neither of those nationalities. Nor is he Spanish.

4

My mind wanders back to the Finnish diplomat, with his pale hair and fresh face. Just a big boy in a suit. Would he feel so warm, the mingling scents of his skin and after-shave be able to send me dizzy? I hardly think so.

And why would anyone be chasing him? He looked too innocent to be capable of any crime. Or was that his foil? Had he accessed the files I'd been meant to copy?

Someone certainly had. Hardly had I typed in the password when security had got there. They already knew someone had cracked the system. But it wasn't me who downloaded the codes.

Or am I on the wrong track? Perhaps the one word he said has been misleading me? So if not Baltic, what might the edge to his accent be? Slavic, maybe?

I suddenly remember the Bulgarian envoy. I'd seen him so briefly I'd forgotten all about him – if anyone could forget such a face. Hardly had we been introduced when that fool of an ambassador dragged me away:

'Melissa, my dear, you must come and help me! Señor Alonso's been talking to me for the past quarter of an hour, and I haven't the foggiest what the chappy wants!'

A small, agitated Spaniard with a thin moustache and slicked-back hair stood waiting hopefully for my assistance. And like a mere apparition, the fleeting glimpse of a god turned mortal, the Bulgarian envoy disappeared from sight. I'd not seen him again all evening. At first too caught up in translating, and then too intent on accomplishing the mission entrusted to me, to realise my loss.

Can it really be him? My heart bounces. Is fortune looking on me kindly? Have I been allowed a second chance? It's too dark to see anything. Even the vaguest outline. How I'd love to reach up into his face and trace its contours. Like a blind person, build his image from the way he feels.

And what would I feel? Soft, wavy hair, I know must be black? The slightest stubble on his hollow cheeks? A straight nose, sleek eyebrows, long eyelashes? Lips inviting my kiss? And can you guess the colour of things by the way they feel? Would I be able to sense his eyes are a rich hazel brown, his skin olive? Would the picture I conjure up do justice to reality? Or would any man perceived this way seem the embodiment of Adonis?

The baying of dogs in the background brings my thoughts back to the danger outside. Immediately he tenses. I cower against him. They're getting closer.

He strokes my hair. 'Shhh!' This time the sound is soft and soothing. I bathe in his breath as the air streams over me. Warm and spicy, with a hint of wine and garlic. Flavours of the Mediterranean.

'They are not looking for you,' he murmurs.

But are they looking for him?

The words were deliberate, his accent heavy. But Bulgarian? Would I know what it sounded like, if I heard it?

I listen to the air passing through his nostrils, feel his rib-cage heave and fall, my cheek bedded on a silk cushion of spice-scented curls.

Do they extend in a stripe down over his stomach I wonder? Disappear beneath the cummerbund, even? Could I stroke the front of his shirt without him noticing, or insert a cautious finger between the buttons, maybe?

God, what am I thinking of? We've got to get out of here.

I lift my head and look into the blackness where his face must be.

'We can't stay here,' I say in an urgent whisper. 'We've got to go on.'

He restrains me as I pull away from him and lightly plants a kiss on my forehead.

'Trust me.'

Trust him? I'm not even sure who he is. A man from the underworld ... and which side is he on? For all I know, I may be colluding with the enemy.

But an enemy who smells so good? Who offers me his warmth and protection ... and makes me ache with want.

He pulls me back against him. Our bodies collide, sending a shock-wave rippling through me, a frisson of excitement riding its wake. He draws in a long deep breath and holds me there, as if trying to prolong the moment. Might he be getting as excited as I am? The static between us tells me the tension's growing. And I don't mean the fear of danger.

My fingers are itching to touch his face and find out if I've guessed his identity. I yearn to know if this man is the thing myths are made of. And if he won't answer me, how else am I supposed to know whose body is so close to mine I can feel every twitch of his muscles?

He slides his hands down over my hips, the black chiffon of my dress scrunching beneath his touch. My heartbeat picks up. For a few seconds anticipation hangs heavy in the air about us. He seems to breathe up my growing arousal and gives a low, deep hum of recognition. And then before I know it, my lips are straining to reach his. And when they unite, any sense of the approaching danger is obliterated.

As we kiss, my hands frenziedly ply the contours of his face, overwhelmed by the need to touch him. To find out who he is. And I'm surprised to find his hair wet at the temples, sticking to him in wisps. Oh yes, he's getting excited! And it hardly matters now who he is, so badly do I want him.

He traces the outline of my face, exploring the fineness of my features. Then his fingers glide down my neck and close round my breasts, already craving his caress.

I'm sucked into a black hole of want. The gnawing emptiness, the stifled longing, the suppressed desire, raw need, surging to the surface. Why have I been wasting my time on a man who has no heart?

I squash myself against his hands, and as he gently squeezes my flesh, a spasm plucks at the pit of my stomach sending an electric shiver through me. I feel the blood drop to my feet. Then an instant later it rises in me with a searing heat, bubbling through my veins, flooding my body with a prickly hotness. I've not felt this warm, this wanted, in ages. Greedily my mouth clutches at his, not wanting any of it to end. Yet I know my passion is folly.

He breaks away. Little kisses land on my neck in a tickling line from my ear-lobe to my collar bone. My mouth tries to snatch at his lips again, but his head descends out of reach, searching out the swelling of my breasts. He licks my flesh where it disappears beneath its chiffon veil. My skin tingles with wetness. Then he finds my nipple, proud and hard, and sucks on it through the material. I have to bite my tongue to stop myself crying out with delight. How I've yearned for this.

My back arches, thrusting the point deeper into his mouth. His other hand works on its twin, gently clamping it between his fingers. And the harder he sucks on one side, the more pressure he applies to the other. Until the tender flesh is burning and the spasms shooting through my stomach soar through me like phosphorus flares.

I'm ablaze. The small cold recess has become a snug dark lair. Both our bodies are pumping out heat, an infra-red glow in the cool empty blackness. I can only hope the guards are not equipped with heat-tracking devices.

He crouches and places his kisses on my stomach, slowly inching lower. Can he feel the tremors inside? Do his lips tingle with the electric current running through me?

I part my legs slightly and he buries his nose in the fabric of my dress where my panties form a little triangle beneath. He breathes me up. A special scent concocted of shower lotion, sweat and the perfume of my own juices. A scent so guaranteed to entice, it should be bottled. And I've not been using it sparingly. The lacy material of my panties is wringing wet.

He nuzzles me, gently rubbing the nub of my clitoris through the two-ply material of my dress: the chiffon and its silky lining. An ideal combination of fabrics for generating prickly sparks of static. The bolts of energy dance through the frilly folds of my vulva, tickling me wickedly, and making the pulsating in my cervix ever more urgent.

Slowly he begins to shimmy my dress up above my hips. Until he reaches the hem and feels the flesh of my thighs above my silk stockings. His fingers feel for the straps of my suspenders. And a little thrill runs through me when I hear him purr with gratification on finding the lace-trimmed strips of elastic. What is it about suspender belts that so turns men on?

He kisses my trembling flesh above the stocking tops. First on the outside of my leg, then on the inside where the skin is so tender. And soon his kisses have reached

9

the triangle of my panties and his tongue has found my clitoris, teasing it through the lace. I'm crying out for more, and harder, and pull his head against me. Playfully his teeth nip my flesh, until neither I nor he can stand it any more. Swiftly he rolls the material down far enough for his mouth to close round the bud of my clitoris … and sucks.

Never have I experienced the pull on my womb with such intensity. The tugging spasms are almost too much to bear. A low ache that is more pain than pleasure. Until it vibrates through me in a rippling wave of contractions that set my womb humming and cervix pulsating in rapture.

Why has no one ever done this to me before? How does he know this is what I crave, when no other lover has ever come close to guessing? I was wrong – he is the Devil! This is far too good to be anything allowed on earth.

And it doesn't stop there – soon his tongue is weaving little circles around the swollen flesh. He licks and caresses me, travelling deeper into the cavern between my legs. Tasting my flesh, lapping up my juices.

And then suddenly this no longer seems to satisfy him. He pulls me hard against his cheek, my delicate flesh scratching against the stubble of his beard. Delicious friction. His hands roughly take hold of my half-bare buttocks, his thumbs hooking over the rolled top of my panties, and in one swift swish he pulls them right down to my knees.

My stomach is aflutter. What's he got in store for me next? Can he take me any higher? Haven't I just been to heaven?

His head moves away. I feel his hands guide the rolled up lacy fabric to my ankles. He helps me step out of them, and stuffs them into a pocket of the coat I'm wearing. Otherwise they'd be lost.

Slowly he stands. Slightly dizzy. His hands using my body to steady himself. When he draws me close to him, his erection presses hard into my stomach.

Gently I rub the tip of his shaft through his trousers. He lets out a low moan. Helpless in his pleasure.

And the moment he moans, I hear the whining of the dogs outside. Torch-light penetrates the first few yards of blackness. Men's voices shout instructions to one another. Suddenly the darkness is teeming with sounds and movement.

Surely the guards can't have found us yet? There must be time for me to work on my unknown lover, reward him for the pleasure he's given me? Let there be a few seconds left before discovery!

My fingers scramble over the satin folds of the cummerbund to the flies of his trousers. Hurriedly I unzip them, free him of their confinement. His cock is hard and straight, begging to be fondled.

Just a few squeezes, surely? Or is there time for me to crouch and close my mouth round its delicate end?

But hardly have my fingers started to stroke him, than he roughly brushes my hand away. He doesn't seem to want it.

There's no time for disappointment. Heavy boots crunch into the dark. A dog whines. The metal clip joining collar and lead snap together. There's a growl from the guard, the hiss of a whiplash on flanks, a yelp. All sounds magnified and echoing about us. Fear tugs at my throat and is answered in the dog's pitiful whimper.

The end is upon us. It's only a matter of some thirty seconds now before we're caught. I can hardly bear the waiting.

And my lover, too, is choking his impatience.

Swiftly he lifts me from the ground and presses me against the wall. There's no fumbling, no dallying, and the darkness is irrelevant. His cock penetrates me as if equipped with some homing device. I hardly have time to gasp in surprise and delight.

This is sheer madness.

The guard is now just a few paces beyond this cold curtain of blackness.

My lover's panting will give us away.

Yet I don't try to stop him.

His hips thrust against mine, bruising my skin in his urgency. My fingers grasp the back of his neck, my knees and thighs grip him as if he were a horse I'm riding. The muscles of my inner walls clasp his penis as though this is the place I'm holding on the tightest.

The only thing that matters is the moment. And this is a moment I don't want to miss, whatever fate is waiting for me afterwards.

Time and again his cock slides into me as he hammers me into the wall, my back mercifully cushioned by the thick coat. As my body absorbs the shock of his thrusts, spasms again shoot through my cervix. A pulsating that sends delicious ripples right through me. A sensation that grows in intensity until it renders me helpless and exhausted, lost in pleasure.

My head's spinning. I no longer know whether I'm standing or lying down. In this blackness there are no points of reference. My sense of sight is defunct. But as in the blind, my other senses overcompensate for its loss.

His big, warm hands pawing my body seem red-hot. The dank atmosphere about us is perfumed with the heady spices of his skin and after-shave, released in a mist of evaporating sweat. And I can taste the salt, like you can taste sea air. And his kisses? An inebriating mixture of him and my own body's perfumes.

Round and round my head swirls. Higher and higher the spasms of pleasure spiral. My whole body is a spinning mass of trembling flesh. I'm awash with waves of ecstasy. Tides that roll over me one after the other. Is there no end to it? This whirling is sending me dizzy.

And the fear of discovery only heightens my enjoyment. The guard is but a few steps away. A blind spectator to our love-making. I can hear his heavy breathing, the whimper of his dog, smell wet fur and sweat. I'm electrified. A kind of inverse voyeuristic satisfaction. He can see nothing of what he witnesses. While I, the object of his clandestine pleasure, know he's watching.

With a final thrust and a low moan of complete ecstasy, my lover sinks against me. I hold him to me, heavy and limp, while the spasms still ring through my body.

In the background there's a long, hoarse sigh. Then, after a few moments, I hear words of reassurance whispered to the dog and the soft crunch of retreating footsteps.

Did he just think he'd stumbled upon two lovers? Why didn't he shine his torch in our faces? Or was what we did for him worth more than a pat on the back from his superiors?

And what about the others? Were their dogs afraid of the dark? Had they refused to go any deeper into the tunnel? And were the men, without their dogs, less courageous than their uniforms implied?

Gradually the spasms ebb away while my lover regains his strength. Around us there is only darkness. And total silence.

I can hardly believe we've got away.

And what now? Should we slink back to the old mansion house, enter its grounds by different paths? Or brazenly return together, flaunting our liaison?

And why not? What better way of deflecting suspicion from one-another? Our own alibis. Obliviously indulging in private pleasures when at the Old Hall all hell broke loose. Deliriously unaware of all that has happened since.

And what crueller way could I ever devise of telling my cold-hearted lover he's been forsaken for a stranger, his mission abandoned.

I shiver with the thrill of it. He was a man of dubious honesty. So have I made the descent into the underworld, the fall has not been far.

Love's envoy stirs in my arms. I kiss his sweat-streaked cheek and drape the coat flaps round him. He pulls out of me and I use my panties to wipe him clean. Hand in hand we pick our way through the darkness.

When we reach the mouth of the tunnel, the moon makes a halo of his pale hair.

After Dark
by Elizabeth Cage

'A computer training course in Basingstoke isn't exactly my idea of a good time,' I complained to my friend Caz.

'Stop moaning, Mira. You might meet some nice people.'

She always saw the positive side of everything. I wish I had her outlook. But I was annoyed at having to miss the speed dating night at a local hotel planned for Thursday, followed by a trip to my favourite club. A group of us were going to go, and it would have been a right laugh. The computer course ran over two days so I had to stay away overnight.

'There'll be other nights out,' Caz remarked. 'And at least you get the hotel paid for.'

'Hotel? That's a joke. My employer does everything on the cheap, so it's a travel motel for me. No luxury perks like a gym and pool.'

'Don't whinge. Anyway, you can text me when you get there, tell me all about it.'

'Yeah, great. And you can tell me all about the fun you're having while I'm eating a sad meal all alone in the Beefeater next to the motel.'

It didn't help that I hated my job right now, so I wasn't exactly feeling motivated to undertake a boring training course for their benefit. But there was no escape, so I duly printed off a map and directions and set off the night before the course so I would avoid the rush hour the next day on the motorways. It was pouring with rain and I managed to get lost twice. I arrived in a foul mood and went to the check-in desk.

'Your room is on the ground floor,' said the female receptionist without smiling.

'Oh, I thought single females were put on the first floor, for security reasons. That's what it says on your website.'

'Unfortunately we are fully booked. This is the only room available.'

I wasn't pleased but took the key. I needed to get warm and dry. The room was down a long corridor, quite nice, spacious, and had all I needed – TV, hairdryer, kettle, etc. But the motel was set in a big leisure park, with a cinema and restaurants, and peering out of my window it seemed to me it would be easy for someone to break in through it. I didn't feel very safe somehow, especially as I couldn't make the door lock properly. While I ran a bath, I wedged a chair up against the door, just in case.

The bath relaxed me, and it felt good to lie back and soak in the hot, scented, bubbly water. I started to doze off and was woken by the sound of loud voices and footsteps in the corridor. Noisy guests. I hoped it wouldn't be like that all evening.

I dried off, got into the bed and switched the TV on, but I felt restless. I texted Caz to see what she was up to, but she didn't reply, so I figured she was out for the night – probably having a lot more fun than me, though that wouldn't have been difficult. Feeling aggrieved, I flicked through the channels before turning the TV off. I decided to leave the light on all night, just a bedside lamp, as I still felt nervous. There was, however, a foolproof way that I knew would relax my mind and body and get me off to sleep.

Reaching into my bag, I took out my favourite pink vibe and smiled. I had put new batteries in, anticipating that it would be well used for the next two nights. I sighed and slipped it between my thighs so the tip was resting gently on my clit. I switched it on, the slowest setting first, and savoured the gentle vibrations. It usually never took long with my faithful friend. By the time I was at level three, I was groaning with delight, the sensations pulsating though me, creating wonderful waves of pure pleasure. Bliss. I came several times, losing count as I drifted off into a peaceful, satisfied slumber.

However, this was short-lived. I was abruptly awoken in the early hours by a loud crashing noise. Thinking I was still dreaming, I half roused myself, my senses dulled by sleep. Then my brain kicked into gear and I realised it was the sound of a chair falling over. I got up, not fully awake yet, but aware that something was not right. Stumbling out of the bed, I was horrified to see that the door was open. My heart missed a beat when I saw a figure outlined there. It was a man. I was so shocked I was unable to scream. I just stood there in my flimsy short T-shirt.

We stared at each other in dazed silence. Then he said, 'Please excuse me.' He looked as scared as me. 'I'm so sorry.' His voice was soft and mellow. I wondered how a guest could get into the wrong room by mistake. Surely all the keys were different? Then the door closed and he was gone. I stood aghast, trembling.

It was like a bad dream, a situation that, living alone in my cosy flat, I had always dreaded. I sat down by the phone, considering what to do next. Would he come back? What if he was a prowler? It took me a good ten minutes to compose myself. Then I picked up the phone, hands shaking, and rang the motel's night desk.

'Hello. I want to report an intruder in my room. A man just tried to get in.'

'Yes, madam. I know.' The voice was unnervingly familiar. 'It was me.'

I went silent. This was totally unexpected. I didn't know what to think.

'I'm the night porter. I cannot apologise enough. I assure you this sort of thing has never happened before. I'm so sorry.'

'I couldn't lock the door,' I muttered numbly. I felt very vulnerable.

'There was a mix-up on the computer. We had a late arrival and I thought your room was empty,' he explained. 'I know that probably sounds unlikely to you right now, but believe me, it's the truth.'

'You scared me.'

'I would offer to re-room you but we are fully booked. You will, of course, receive a full refund.'

I considered packing my stuff, getting in my car and driving back home. But it was 1 a.m., bitterly cold and raining outside and I was tired.

'At least let me fix the lock on your door,' he offered. 'Hopefully that might make you feel a bit safer.'

'OK.' It still felt unreal.

While I waited, wrapping myself in a big white fluffy bathrobe, I texted Caz to tell her what had happened. Just in case …

There was a timid knock on the door. I opened it carefully. He looked very sheepish. The night porter was in his early thirties, like me, and had warm brown eyes and soft dark hair.

'I'm really sorry about what happened earlier,' he said again. He seemed genuine and I felt more reassured. I noticed he was wearing a rather smart charcoal grey uniform. I had a thing for uniforms. He was also carrying a tool bag. I like a man with a good set of tools. I had often watched my rather attractive neighbour working on his car, and when the plumber came round, I liked to watch him too. There was something sexy about a man who knew how to handle his tools. Call me pervy, but it turned me on. A lot.

'Can I come in?' he asked cautiously.

'Of course.'

I studied his strong arms and hands as he took out a screwdriver and set to work on the lock. Long, slim fingers. Mmmmm.

When he had finished he turned to me and said, 'There, all fixed. You should have no more unwelcome visitors now.'

'Thank you.' I paused. 'Would you like a cuppa?'

He shook his head. 'Not allowed. Anyway, I've caused you enough bother. I have to get back to work.'

'At least stay with me a while longer,' I insisted. 'Until I feel less anxious.'

It was a lie. Now I had spoken properly to him I felt surprisingly safe. If the truth be told, I was actually feeling quite aroused. The distinctive uniform he was wearing with the golden trim and shiny buttons, his set of tools ... And the clincher ... the huge bunch of heavy silvery keys on his belt that jangled when he moved. Caz had often teased me about my fetish. It was both the sight of them – they were shiny – and the sound they made. Keys meant power. Power was sexy.

I gestured for him to sit by me on the edge of the bed.

Now it was his turn to be anxious. His shoulder brushed against mine for the briefest of moments but it was enough to set my pulse racing. He glanced nervously at the bedside table and I wondered what he thought about the big pink vibe sitting there. I had forgotten to put it away. Oops.

'I really should be going now,' he began again.

'Are you sure? I would like you to stay with me. Just a little longer.'

'You'll get me into trouble.' But his face was so close now, I could feel his breath on my neck.

'Please?' I leaned over and kissed him. He didn't pull away. At first, he let me caress his mouth with my lips and tongue, simply receiving the pleasure, but soon he was returning my attention, tentatively at first, then greedier until his passion matched my own. I let my bathrobe slip from my shoulders and his hands found my breasts, kneading and exploring my nipples through the thin fabric of my T-shirt. Slowly, he pushed me back onto the bed, lifting my T-shirt up over my head. He tossed it onto the carpet. God, I wanted him. In his uniform. As he started to unbutton his smart jacket I whispered, 'No, leave it on.'

I reached out and grabbed the bunch of keys on his leather belt, fingering and caressing them suggestively. Seeing this, he unhooked them from his belt and dangled them over my mouth, letting them stroke my lips. I licked and sucked the hard metal. He smiled, before slowly running them across my naked body, inch by inch, taking his time, lingering on my breasts and nipples. I trembled with delight at their coldness, although they soon picked up my body heat. He continued to track them down my belly towards my thighs. I shuddered with delighted anticipation as he rested them between my legs. It felt like a jolt of electricity was passing through my clit. Unable to control myself, I cried out. To stifle the sound, he covered my open mouth with his, kissing me hard, using his tongue. After a long, passionate kiss he looked into my eyes and murmured, 'Shhh,' resting one finger across my mouth.

By now my clit was so wet I could almost taste it. The smell of my juices on the sheets was overpowering. Gradually, and very gently, he pushed the largest of the keys into my opening. I gasped. While he moved it slowly from side to side, he also exerted the lightest fingertip pressure on my clit. I was melting. The combination of the hard metal and his sensitive fingering brought me quickly to the edge. Before I knew what was happening, I had come, intensely and abruptly.

He removed the key, placed it in his mouth and sucked it clean of my juices before clipping it back on his belt to join the others. My heart was racing but he continued to tantalise my helpless juicy clit, muffling my groans and whimpers with his left hand now, lowering his head to nibble and nip my exposed breasts as I wriggled and moaned, close to coming again. When he felt my muscles tensing, he took his fingers away and I bit his hand, squealing with frustration.

'Noisy bitch,' he whispered, grabbing my vibe from the bedside table. I thrust my eager wet pussy towards it, writhing, hips arched. It had only been buzzing inside me for seconds before my clit exploded once more. He licked my favourite toy, the way he had the keys.

As I lay there, still reeling, he straddled me, unzipped his flies and pushed his rigid cock into my mouth. He pumped me vigorously, without mercy, and just when I thought I would suffocate, it was his turn to explode. I thought I would choke, there was so much hot sticky fluid, but when he withdrew he put his hand over my mouth and murmured gruffly, 'Swallow, slut. All of it.'

I did.

He rolled off and lay beside me, stroking my tousled hair with his long fingers, kissing the nape of my neck. I felt dizzy. And very tired.

When I awoke, many hours later, I was alone. The duvet had been pulled over me so I wouldn't get cold. My vibe was sitting innocently on the bedside table, as if it had never been moved. I snuggled up in the warm bed, reluctant to move. Unfortunately I had a computer course to go to. Glancing at my travel alarm clock, I sighed. Time to get up.

As I soaped myself in the shower, I wondered if it had all been a dream. A vivid, horny dream.

I listened to the news on breakfast television, dressed and picked up my bag. As I opened the door, I noticed something poking out underneath it. A white envelope. I bent down and picked it up. It felt hard. Tearing it open, I was surprised to find a key. A big, shiny key. And a yellow Post-it note with a room number and the words, 'Guess who's on duty again tonight?'

I smiled. Maybe my stay in Basingstoke wouldn't be so uneventful after all.

Housemate Potential
by Penelope Friday

The Harley's engine went from a loud roar to a dull murmur and then silence as it came to a standstill. Rob swung one leather-clad leg after another from the bike, checked the number of the house and walked firmly up the path. This was the right house, the place advertising for a housemate.

The door opened just as Rob got to it. The guy was around Rob's height (an inch or so under six foot), with blond hair and an uncertain smile.

'I'm here about the room.'

'Sorry?' he said vaguely.

Rob stripped the gloves from long-fingered hands, and pushed the helmet up. Blond guy looked – glanced away – looked again – as Rob's dark hair tumbled down onto her shoulders.

'Oh. You're ... um ...'

'Very tall for a woman,' Rob supplied drily.

'Yeah,' he said weakly.

She watched him glance over her body, knowing that he was looking for the signs that should have told him before that she was female: pausing a second on the snug leather jacket that hinted at her small rounded breasts before slipping lower. She allowed her own eyes to do

23

the same, and was made aware that he was not displeased by what he saw.

'The room?' she pressed again.

'Oh yeah. I'm Alex, by the way.'

'Rob.'

He half held out a hand, then dropped it as he realised that her hands were full with her helmet and gloves.

'Do you want to leave these down here? They'll be quite safe.'

Rob piled her things neatly on the dresser by the door and followed him towards the staircase.

'It's up here.'

Rob saw with amusement that he was having difficulty keeping his eyes off her. Presumably when he advertised for a housemate, a six-foot biker girl had not been his imagined respondent. All the same ... he didn't seem precisely upset. She followed close behind him on the stairs, making sure that he was ever aware of her presence, of her closeness – of her femininity.

'Have you lived here long?' she murmured.

He jumped. Physically jumped. Rob bit back a smile: she oughtn't to be doing this, but it was too tempting. He was too *aware* of her.

'N-no ...' He paused. 'No, I haven't,' he said more collectedly.

'Chatty, aren't you?'

They'd reached the top of the stairs. He turned round to her and gave the apologetic smile again. 'You ... er ... disconcert me.'

Rob raised an eyebrow.

'Not much contact with women?'

'Not with women like you.' He clearly regretted it the minute he said it, blushing a deep crimson that spread from his face to his neck.

Again, Rob was forced to swallow her grin. Was this boy really as innocent as he seemed? Surely no one could be that naive? She wouldn't mind discovering, either way.

'So show me the bedroom,' she invited.

She heard his sharp intake of breath, but kept her eyes coolly fixed on his face, expression neutral. If he wanted, well, what it seemed like he wanted, he would have to make it clearer than this. And as the throb began to start between her thighs ... she hoped that he would show her precisely what he needed.

'Through here.'

She brushed against him as they moved through the doorway into the small room, which was dominated by a double bed. He was still aroused: she could feel it, could hear the still uncertain breathing that showed his interest. Let him wait. Let him wait and wonder.

'Nice decor.'

The sarcasm was clear but not unkind. The room appeared to have been last decorated in the 1970s; psychedelic flowered wallpaper gave the room a claustrophobic edge. It made the mind spin as if delirious ... made people act in ways perhaps unusual to them.

It was perfect.

'Um ... you – I mean, whoever moves in – could always redecorate,' Alex said.

She was standing just behind him.

'But do you think you'd like my way of redecorating?' she whispered in his ear.

He turned his head, fast, to look at her. Their similarity in height was at its most obvious now. Their eyes were on the same level – and so were their mouths.

Rob waited.

'I ...' Alex leaned forward and kissed her mouth, but he was still uncertain, Rob thought with amusement. What did he think she'd do to him? What – her heart rate quickened and she increased the pressure of their kiss – did he *hope* she'd do to him? She moved away and looked at him thoughtfully. His eyes had shut when they kissed, but she had kept hers open, wanting to use every sense available.

'I think I might,' he muttered. 'Like it your way, I mean.'

'That sounds promising.'

Rob pulled the zip of her jacket down slowly, still keeping her eyes on Alex. She shrugged her shoulders out of it, and the leather creaked slightly as she pulled her arms out.

'Hot in here, isn't it?' she said conversationally.

'Um ...'

'Likely to get hotter, do you think?'

'I don't know.' But his breathing, she noted, was irregular.

'I've always liked it hot. You?'

'Depends where I am.'

And how out of your depth you are, thought Rob. Alex was hesitant – very hesitant – but definitely not unwilling. Guiding him through, introducing him to new experiences, would be particularly satisfying. She would be kind (of course), and although she couldn't guarantee it, she intended him nothing but pleasure. On her terms, obviously: that much was understood.

She ran a hand across the back of her neck, underneath the cascade of brown hair. 'Are you hot?'

'Warm,' he admitted.

'It's that jumper. Let me help you off with it.'

Rob slid her hands underneath the jumper. He was wearing a thin cotton shirt, and she could feel his muscles through the material. She slid her hands upwards, taking the jumper with them; he bent his head to allow her to pull the material free.

'Is that better?'

'I guess,' he answered.

'Good.'

If he was intending to wait for her to make all the moves, he was going to be sorely disappointed. He would have to work for his pleasure.

She sat down on the bed and took another look around the bedroom.

'A large bed for the size of room, isn't it?' she suggested.

'People seem to prefer it,' he said uncomfortably, his eyes anywhere but on her face. 'They like to have room.'

'Room for what?'

'Well, whatever, really, I guess.'

'And is there room enough for you here?'

He looked at her, scanning her body in an embarrassed fashion. Was he going to take the opportunity or not? Rob still wasn't certain, which made it all the more interesting. He'd *like* to, she was sure of that – but his inhibitions were strong. There was a long uncomfortable silence that she made no move to break. Then: 'Yeah,' he said at last. 'At least, I think so. And you?'

'And me.' She reached out and stroked a hand down his thigh. 'Why don't you come and sit down?'

He obeyed. Rob was pleased. Alex might be shy, but he knew what he wanted. If they were lucky, their wants might even overlap. She leaned down to undo her bootlaces, and felt a warm dry hand on her arm.

27

'Let me.' It was more a request than an instruction; and the pink flush was again on his cheeks.

She raised her eyebrows. Well, at any rate he seemed to be a quick learner. This might be even better than she had imagined! Lazily, she lifted a leg and placed one booted foot on his lap. Her boot was too solid to give her a good impression of his state of arousal, but he seemed keen enough. His fingers were slow but certain as he pulled the laces apart and slipped the first boot from her foot. She could feel his erection now, and she rubbed the sole of her foot suggestively against the bulge in his trousers.

'You're good,' she approved.

'The other foot?' He was biting back his stammer in every word, his excitement obvious.

She lifted her other foot over the first so that her feet were crossed. While he pulled at the fastenings of her left boot, she continued to move her right foot slowly and sensuously against him. His hands were more unsteady now: she had distracted him too much.

'Why don't you undress?' she asked lazily. 'I do believe the temperature is beginning to rise a little, don't you?'

'Mmm, it is warm.'

She jerked her head towards the middle of the room, and he stood up.

'Um ...?'

'Start with your shirt,' she advised. 'Work your way down.'

He nodded and raised his hands to the top button. Rob could see that he was trying not to rush, yet at the same time was finding it hard to control his impatience. She lay back on the bed, her head resting on one hand, and watched in silence. When the shirt had fallen to his feet he hesitated for a second, and gave her a quick glance.

'Belt,' she said briefly. 'Then trousers. And take your socks off.'

He undressed nervously, and she read his mind.

'Don't worry. You won't disappoint.'

Not if the feeling between her legs was anything to go by. The very *thought* of taking him was turning her on. She ran a hand across her front, feeling the hard nipples through the thick material. He would be able to see the peaks, to know that she wanted this. Perhaps it would reassure him.

When he was standing naked in front of her she beckoned him over and kissed him again.

'My turn now.'

She pulled him down so that he was on the bed beside her, and then she stood up.

'Let me tell you something, Alex,' she said huskily, noting the look of eager frustration on his face. 'The anticipation adds to the event itself. You may be sure of that.'

Her tongue flickered round her lips, wetting them and leaving them glistening with moisture. Her red top was whisked over her head, and thrown casually to the floor. She wore no bra. Her hands went deliberately to the button on her leather trousers and then paused. Alex's hand had slipped down and he was touching himself with a desperate need.

'Hands off,' she said sharply. 'No cheating.'

'But ...'

She stood absolutely still, hands waiting at the waist of her trousers, exposed from that point upwards. Now was the time to discover whether he was really prepared to learn. He pouted – positively, he pouted – but his hand dropped to his side as she had demanded.

29

'Good boy.'

She had teased him enough, Rob thought. The trousers were tight, and they needed a firm hand to slip them down her legs, along with the black, delicate knickers that she was wearing underneath. She was aware that he could not look away from her, and she enjoyed the sense of power that he was prepared to give her.

'I'm looking forward to this,' she said gently. 'Are you?'

'I think so.'

Alex's hand was slipping towards his cock once more.

'I've got a better idea.'

Rob knelt in front of him and opened her mouth, allowing him to slide into its wet depths. She moved slowly, deliberately, making sure that he was aware of every millimetre of movement. She breathed in deeply, revelling in the masculine odour: he was clean, yet musky scented.

'You taste good,' she said as she lifted her head, her tongue curling once more around her lips. 'How do you feel?'

His eyes were shut and he had thrust an arm across his face and was biting into the soft flesh of his arm to prevent himself from moaning aloud. Rob smiled as she got to her feet.

'Let me find out what you feel like,' she said suggestively.

She pushed him on to his back, her hands around his wrists. She forced his arms either side of his head and stood over him, looking down on his body. He was in good shape. His muscles were clearly defined, and the light spattering of gold-blond hair across his chest tempted her to put her mouth to it.

'Do you want me?'

He mumbled something that might have been acquiescence, but Rob wanted a firm confirmation. She would not allow him to suggest that he had not been, at all times, a willing – more than willing – partner.

'Do you want me?' she asked again, a steely note in her voice.

'You know I do.'

'That's all I wanted to hear.'

She positioned herself over him and guided him inside her, before returning her hands to their vice-like grip on his arms.

'You do feel good,' she mused aloud.

'Rob ...'

'Uh-huh?'

He was trying to move from his position underneath her, but she wouldn't allow that. She was in control; it was she who would make the moves. She always did – at least, these days.

'Oh, you want more?' she asked.

'Rob ...!'

She moved, rocking back and forth on top of him, her eyes open. She could hear his urgent breathing, the small groaning sound in each breath he took. Her own breath was coming faster now; she could feel her heart pounding in her chest. Fast, fast, faster – the movement was all-consuming, all-important; she had no desire to tease him any more, just to continue to move, to reach the moment of climax.

He came first, and the pulse of his orgasm triggered hers. She heard, as if from a distance, him groan out her name in his pleasure: her own climax was as always

31

silent, private, unshared.

She lay on top of him as she tried to regain her breath, to re-master herself. Then, as he was still gasping, she stood and dressed.

'Let me know about the room,' she said as she left.

'I'll call you,' Alex said breathlessly.

Rob wondered if he would ...

The Secret Whore
by Sadie Wolf

My name is Caroline, and I am thirty years old. I'm not the kind of woman who turns heads in the street, but that's because I prefer not to attract that kind of attention. Most of the time I wear comfortable jeans and T-shirts and no make-up, and although I have long, honey-coloured hair, most of the time I wear it tied back. I'm the one who prefers a quiet night in to a night down the pub, and when I do go out I'll be the one in the corner hiding behind a G&T.

My husband Steve is the outgoing one. He's the manager at a windows company, so he's used to being around lots of people, and coping with shop floor banter. He's the one who'll tell jokes down the pub and revels in being the centre of attention. Even after a long day at work, he'll still come home chatty and cheerful.

I like to cook, and every day without fail I'll be in the kitchen with my apron on, cooking our tea. There'll always be a homemade cake in the cake tin and if it's anybody's birthday I'll always bake them a cake. Like I said, Steve's a cheerful man, and when he comes home I'll make us a cup of tea and he'll give me a kiss, and we'll eat at the table and swap stories about our days. He always has some funny story about what the lads and lasses from work have been up to. I work part time, and if I've been at work I'll tell him something about what the girls have been up to, or complain about what a muddle the accounts were in, if I've had a difficult kind of day. If I haven't been at work, there'll always be something to tell him, about what I've seen at the shops, or who I've seen. I spend a lot of time on the housework, because I think that's important, but I always make sure I've got something interesting to talk about: I wouldn't want him to get bored of me.

After tea he'll watch some TV, or go on the computer, and I'll tidy up, do the dishes and then I'll sit down with a book, or do a bit of cross-stitch. We look to all the world like a nice, normal couple. We'll be in bed by half past ten, as Steve has to be in work by eight. We have sex about once a week, usually on a Saturday or Sunday morning, unless we've been down the pub, or he has, and then it might be an extra time. I guess that's about average for a couple that has been married five years.

I suppose some wives, most, probably, could content themselves with this life. It's not as if I've got anything to complain about – nice house, two good holidays a year, no money worries. I've come to the conclusion that it's just me, something about the way I've been wired, something uniquely peculiar about my temperament.

How else do I explain the fact that for the last two years I have been selling myself three days a week at a brothel in town?

I start at eight in the morning, doing a bit of cleaning and helping with the accounts. It's much easier for me that way, when I need to talk about what I do. Clients tend to come in from about eleven, then there's a busy period over lunchtime, and then I leave off at three. Mind you, you'd be surprised, sometimes people ring in and make appointments for eight in the morning, on the way to work, can you imagine! Well, I can, it's the secrecy I suppose, going into work knowing something no one else does, doing something no one else does.

After two years, I've got a few regulars: nice easy work, like having a few extra husbands. They're mostly older, long-term married. I think they come to see me as a way to stop them from getting divorced, so in some ways maybe I'm doing their poor wives a favour. Like I said, on the whole, the regulars are easy. It's the strangers who really excite me.

We're quite safe, the boss runs a tight ship, we've got panic buttons and Julie, our receptionist, has got an eye and an ear for the funny ones; but there's still a thrill of danger the first time you take a stranger into a room. If I'd had more guts I'd have tried streetwalking. I know that sounds ridiculous, why would anyone choose that, but there's just something so exciting about a stranger's car pulling up beside you.

When I first met Steve and we swapped fantasies, like new couples do, I told him about that one. One evening I dressed up in a miniskirt and stockings and a faux-fur coat and stood shivering round the corner from our house. He drove the car round and pulled up and opened the door, like we'd rehearsed, and asked me how much, and I told him twenty quid and he gave it to me. He drove me out of town, along the main road to a lay-by. He'd pulled the passenger seat back, climbed on top of me and fucked me. There wasn't a lot of room, he kept knocking the steering wheel, and I had my feet up on the dashboard. I remember that bit the best, my silver sandals up against the windscreen, catching the light from the passing cars. It had been a little slice of heaven that I'd never forgotten, but he had been sullen and uncommunicative when I tried to talk about it afterwards. It made him feel ashamed, I think. Everyone has their baser urges, but most people would rather just bury them and carry on as if they didn't.

The strangers are often quite shy. There's no haggling over money to break the ice – they pay by the hour at the desk – so when they walk into my room it feels like bringing back a bloke you've just met on a night out. Except that it's the middle of the day and you're stone-cold sober. There's always a slightly awkward pause, when the door closes on the two of you. The boss trained us, and what we have to say to ourselves is: *This is my boyfriend of six months whom I love dearly. We haven't seen each other for a month* ... I say husband, of course, and I try to remember when Steve went away for two weeks on a training course and how excited I was when he came home. I usually just say hi, and put my arms around them, and kiss them like a girlfriend would. They like this, especially if it's their first time, because a lot of people think that working girls don't kiss their clients. Some do, some don't. I do. It's all part of the service. The young men who have come as part of a dare, often drunk after a stag do, they're the most nervous. They don't come back. It's just something they do as a rite of passage, I guess, and besides, most young men haven't got the money to make a habit of it.

I enjoy making myself look nice for the clients, and it's also a good way of getting rid of some of the money I earn. I get my hair cut and coloured every six weeks, blow dried once a week; then there's waxing, facials, nice make-up and so on, and underwear. Of course, most men can't tell the difference between a bra that costs ten pounds and one that costs a hundred pounds, but they know what they like, and I enjoy seeing the look of appreciation on their faces when they first walk into the room.

Ninety-nine per cent of them just want to have normal, straight sex like they would with their girlfriends. Most of them like to have a kiss and a cuddle and a bit of a chat, and I'm good at putting people at their ease. You learn a lot about life, listening to other people's stories. Even though they've paid by the hour, they're often happy to take it slow, and when they do tentatively put out a hand and touch my breast, they look almost surprised that I don't tell them off. I think a lot of them have tried going to those lap dancing clubs, where it's all sit on your hands and don't touch, when for a bit more money than they'd spend on a night out in one of those places, they get to have the complete package.

I like watching the expression on their faces as they let their hands wander, stroking and squeezing and exploring. I usually help them with the bra catch, as most men are all fingers and thumbs. They tend to spend a long time on my breasts, kissing them, holding them, sucking on my nipples like babies. I hold them, and stroke their hair, and tell them how good it feels. And when they are ready, they climb on top of me. Honest to God, I love feeling them enter me, feeling a stranger's penis going into me for the first time. Because there's nothing like the first time, is there? It's the first time that man's been in you, and once he has, he's had you, and that can't ever be undone. And that's why, I think, I like the strangers best, because I like to say to myself, that's another one, I've been had by another one today. It's not like I keep a count or anything, it's just that sense of being available to men, and them wanting me, and having me. Like I say, I'm wired differently from most.

Most of my regulars are easy, and most clients just want ordinary, straight sex, but as everyone knows, it's the exception that proves the rule.

There are two professional guys, both in their mid thirties, both with steady girlfriends, who come and see me together, every month, and have done for the last year or so. I have had men come in pairs before, usually the stag night lads, but they only usually do it once. These two are different. One of them is blond and freckly and big built, and the other's small, with black hair and olive skin, and stubble.

The first time, I sat them down and asked them what they wanted, which is a good way of setting the ground rules, important for safety when you have two of them. The blond one just said something like, oh, you know, just the usual, but the dark one said he just wanted to watch. I wondered if they were gay, or bisexual, or something, but I don't know anymore. It scared me a bit, the first time, the way the dark one just sat there and stared the whole time. He never spoke, never moved. I kept expecting him to suddenly leap to his feet and join in, or do something, but he just sat there.

I liked the blond one – Mike – from the start. He was funny, in a self-deprecating way; he made light of it all, like I imagine he would with a regular woman. He called me darling, and made jokes, in a way that demonstrated respect and nice manners. He didn't seem to mind, or even notice, his friend sitting silent in the chair.

The first time, he was a bit nervous, like all of them. I took the initiative, going down on him straight away, and getting on top of him. He was appreciative and polite, but all the while his friend sat and watched us, and didn't move a muscle. I thought that would be the last I saw of either of them, but they turned up again a month later.

Mike was a lot more relaxed the second time and took control, positioning himself on top of me when he wanted me to suck him, and rolling me over when he was ready to fuck me. He went down on me, and made me genuinely wet. It was good, feeling his bulky body on me, and I felt comfortable with him. His friend – Tom – still sat there, which surprised me, as Mike and I must have looked pretty good together, and I couldn't believe he didn't want some. I caught his eye once or twice, while Mike and I were fucking, but he just stared at me impassively, as if we were doing nothing at all.

They continued visiting every month, and Mike and I got better and better. I felt relaxed with him and he seemed to enjoy my company. We chatted a bit, and he told me he had a girlfriend he lived with, and so did Tom, and that it was officially poker night as far as the girlfriends were concerned. Apparently the girlfriends were quite disapproving of the idea of playing poker, and I got the impression that they were quite prim and proper type girls.

On the sixth visit, Mike asked me if he could have anal sex with me. I lay face down, flat on the bed, and he climbed on top of me. He was lovely and gentle, but it's never the most comfortable experience. Afterwards, I sat up gingerly, and jumped as I saw Tom. He was leaning forward in his chair, his eyes were glittering and his face was filled with such longing that my stomach flipped over. I opened my mouth to speak – I'd never asked him before why he didn't want to join in, or take a turn with me, but I almost did then. But he turned away and picked up his drink, and the moment passed. The time was just about up, in any case, by then, and I felt a bit sorry for him. I wondered what was holding him back. There was something unnerving about the way he had looked at me. Was he shy or inhibited, or was he afraid of giving into his own urges?

Everything changed the next time they came in. Tom had the hungry look that he'd had the time before, and Mike was distant and businesslike. The atmosphere was scary and electric, completely different to usual. Tom sat in his chair, watching, but alive with energy and attention. Mike stood in front of me and unbuttoned his trousers, and I knelt down on the carpet and took his cock in my hand and sucked him. I felt scared, not just of Tom, but of both of them, vulnerable in a way I hadn't felt since their first visit.

'Get undressed.' Mike stepped back and took his trousers and shirt off, while I stood up and undid my bra and took off my knickers. My hands were shaking.

'Get on the bed.' I half lay, half sat on the bed. 'On all fours.' Mike's voice was flat and even, his face expressionless. I glanced for a split second at Tom; his face was glowing with excitement. He spoke: 'Spank her.'

My stomach turned over, and I felt hot between my legs. I felt Mike kneeling on the bed beside me, and then the slap as he brought the flat of his hand down onto my bottom. I held myself as still as I could while he spanked me, and my bottom got hotter and hotter and my skin tingled. I was more excited than scared, then – I liked being spanked, and could cope with the pain.

He stopped spanking me and began fingering me, and I was quite embarrassed about how wet I was. I was so distracted that I practically jumped out of my skin when I saw Tom standing in front of me, his trousers and pants round by his knees, his cock out. His pubic hair was black, and the hair spread onto his stomach and thighs. He was hard and muscular, unlike the soft bulkiness of Mike. His face was set, his jaw clenched. He wasn't looking at me, but behind me, at Mike.

'Do her up the arse,' Tom said.

I felt scared then, of the tone of his voice, and of the way Mike grabbed hold of my hips with no trace of his old gentleness. I felt the tip of his cock pressing up against me, then it being forced inside me. I wanted to lie down, make myself more comfortable, but Mike's hands and forearms were locked around my hips and thighs, and I couldn't move.

He pushed himself all the way in, and I couldn't help it: I cried out. Tom stepped forward and thrust his cock into my mouth. It took all my concentration not to gag as he pushed it in as far as he could, and at the same time, Mike pulled almost all the way out and then pushed in again, forcing his way in all over again. I willed him to stay in, to pull back just a little, and then go in again gently, like he had last time, so that I only had to endure the head of his cock entering me once. Once it was in, it was OK, it was the entering that was the worst, but this time he put me through it again and again at every thrust.

Tom held my hair and forced his way in and out; I wanted to pull back, away from him, but that only pushed me further onto Mike, so I had nowhere to go.

'Swap.' Tom's voice sounded hoarse. I was released, and I whimpered as they let me go. I tried to shift position a little; my knees and legs were aching from holding myself as still as possible. I only had a few seconds reprieve before they started on me again, and this time it was Mike's cock in my mouth, and Tom behind me. They were both faster this time, pushing and thrusting faster and faster, and I knew they were both

41

close to coming. Mike rested his hands on my shoulders and I concentrated on sucking him as nicely as I could, running my tongue over and around the head of his cock, how he liked it. I concentrated hard on keeping up with his rhythm, and it helped distract me from the discomfort I felt from Tom's cock, which was rubbing me and making me sore.

At the same time, Tom filled me up inside in a way that was frightening and exhilarating all at the same time. The tip of his cock touched sensitive areas inside, and although it felt uncomfortable, and even dangerous, to have him fucking me that way, the sensation made me feel like I was going to come. It felt good to be entered that way, it put pressure on different parts of me inside, and being so stretched and so filled up made me feel taken in a way that straight sex couldn't come close to.

I relaxed into Tom then; my body stopped fighting and just allowed it. As I relaxed, I tasted Mike coming in my mouth, and then two seconds later Tom came inside me, and I felt his hands on my hips, drenched in sweat, his thighs wet against me.

They left me on the bed and got dressed. My legs felt wobbly and full of cramp and, undignified as it was, I stayed on all fours for a few moments, waiting for the feeling to return to my legs before I moved.

That was five or six months ago now, and it's been like that ever since. Mike isn't quite as distant as he was, but there's been no return to the friendly banter we used to have. It's as if, since Tom's been actively involved, he sets the tone, and he's always been a bit scary. Or maybe Mike just started seeing me as a whore, instead of a woman, and behaves accordingly. And who can blame him, because, after all, that is what I am.

One day, during a quiet period, I was out the back, doing a bit of dusting and making the beds, when Julie came in.

'Are you ready? I've got someone at the desk. I've not seen him before, but he seems all right. He said he was a regular of Splash, before it got closed down. Said he was gutted about it. So, maybe if you're lucky you'll have a new regular!'

'OK, give me two minutes. Thanks, Julie.'

In my room, I took off my robe and checked myself in the mirror. I was wearing new, outrageously expensive black Agent Provocateur underwear: fifties-style push-up bra, sheer knickers, a suspender belt and black fishnet stockings. I watch what I eat, but I've always had curves, and that style suits me. I brushed my hair, which was past my shoulders and a lovely golden colour, having just been highlighted. I put another coat of lipstick on, dabbed some powder on my cheeks and sprayed myself with perfume. Finally, I slipped into my heels: impossibly high silver stilettos with glass platform heels.

I sat down on the bed and waited, my stomach turning over in excitement and my hands prickling with nerves. I heard footsteps in the hall. I said my mantra in my head, *this is my husband of six months* … even though I didn't need to anymore. The door opened, and Julie's face appeared, and behind her a familiar face, wearing an expression I'd not seen before. It took him a second longer to recognise me, and by the time his face had absorbed the shock, Julie had closed the door on us. I sat on the bed, unable to move or speak. Steve appeared to visibly collect himself. He cleared his throat.

'Well, Caroline, what have we here?' He took off his

jacket, walked over to me and sat down on the bed beside me.

44

Aztec Gold
by Charybdis Childe

Sylvie stumbled on a root as she ran; stumbled, almost fell, managed to keep her balance without slowing. Her heavy walking boots pounded the spongy ground, and tropical leaves and fronds whipped her face as she flew away from the village, her host family and, most of all, away from Joe.

His strong arms and handsome face had entranced her on the shuttle bus at Gatwick. He had noticed her looking and flashed her a perfect smile. By the end of the fourteen-hour flight to Peru she was well and truly besotted. Since then she had spent every possible moment with him. Getting to know each other as they helped to build a new classroom. Laughing together at the differences between there and home. His strong arms around her when she missed her family, being a little sadder than she actually was to savour every moment snuggled against his firm chest. Swiftly the warm days sped by and she allowed herself to luxuriate in them, not needing to rush things, almost sure that he was as into her as she was into him. She was wrong. Innocently spying him in a passionate embrace with a pretty American girl felt like a dagger through the chest. Her legs had responded before she had time to think. And now she was lost in the jungle.

Her pace gradually slowed as she acknowledged her lack of direction. They had been for guided walks through the jungle since they arrived, but none of the scenery seemed familiar. The greenery was increasingly dense, to the point where she had to use her arms to push through walls of leaf and vine. Irritating dribbles of sweat trickled from her hairline and her head ached with the heat. She fought through another thicket of plants and, suddenly, her arms met no resistance. She emerged, clammy and dirty, into a clearing. Opposite her a waterfall shimmered down a vertical stone face, feeding a pool like dark green glass. On one of the jungle walks, a local guide had told them the story of the lost pool of Chalchiuhtlicue. Centuries ago, local rumour maintained, the Incas dedicated a pool to Chalchiuhtlicue, the goddess of water and fertility. The tribes would come and make love to the water, offering their seed as a libation to the goddess. Then one day, against all social law, a young warrior actually dared to penetrate the goddess. Chalchiuhtlicue fell in love with him and together they fled. They were never found. The tribes deserted the sacred pool and today its location is a mystery. No living soul has ever managed to find it.

The jungle surrounding this clearing was all as thick as that which she had just fought through; the place could just have been deserted for centuries. The ground around the water was of the same green stone as the rock face, and deep carvings of spirals and circles surrounded the pool and continued up to the top of the falls. The pool was full to the very brim, so that if a person were to get in, the water would overflow, filling the patterns in the rock. The clearing was flooded with the green smell of water, at once ancient and alive.

Sylvie's hot blood sang in her veins and her skin itched. The sweat still stood on her back and upper lip, and her hair clung where it touched her face. Her eyes on the delicious water, she eased her steaming feet from her walking boots and wriggled her toes on the cool, rough stone. She dragged her vest up over her head, dropped her khaki shorts and clambered out of her knickers. She dove from where she stood, slipping almost silently into the water.

It was curious, as soon as her skin met the water, she found herself incredibly excited. The cool water filtered through the frills of her cunt as they opened happily. She kept her hands away, using the muscles in her thighs to press herself closed, flesh rubbing warm flesh and then relaxing to let the cool water flow through her lips again. The movement became almost meditative, her mind focused totally on the movement back and forth, back and forth.

It was a quiet rustle that brought her back to her senses. She turned in the water to see a figure step through the leaves and up to the water's edge. He stood, his ripples spreading from his ten toes into the centre of the pool. His almond-shaped eyes were the colour of warm treacle and his black hair hung in a loose plait almost to his waist. His slender limbs seemed full of an energy, as though he might spring like a gazelle away into the trees at any moment. He planted his tall spear firmly in the ground and his plump lips pressed together and then relaxed when their eyes met. He was naked apart from a bundle of cloth below his flat, brown stomach, but that did little to disguise his erection. After a moment, he laid his spear on the ground and shamelessly abandoned his cloth. Placing his hands on the ground, he slid feet first into the pool. Modestly, he swam towards her and stopped close to her side, effortlessly treading water. The movements keeping him above water were so slight that the ripples cleared and she could see all of him, the pool bottom far below his undulating feet. His slender mahogany limbs threw her pale curves into womanly contrast. He began to thrust slowly back and forth into the water by her side. Slowly she turned her head to see, anxious that a quick movement could frighten him away. She watched his long erection brazenly rutted in the open space beside her. He was so close she could feel the barely perceptible rise in temperature of the water he stirred with his hot penis. She felt her slit tense in anticipation as he poked and poked his rod towards her, but each time he stopped just before making contact. She found herself gently thrusting the water as well, grateful for the current tickling her eager lips, but yearning for the touch of something more tangible.

e watched his expression change, his liquid eyes narrowing and teeth clenching in a concentrated look of desperation. His hips spasmed and his cock bulged in the final moments. He was in his own personal point of no return, and as a white squirt of liquid twice pierced the water, his fingers grasped at nothing and he let out a small growl of release. She replied with a whimper of her own, heavy with disappointment at the waste of his climax. He focused on her with mild surprise and when she met his eyes, reached forward gingerly to touch her. His fingertips met the sensitive skin of her stomach as though he were expecting them to go straight through her. From his face he seemed pleased that they hadn't. Then he held her more firmly, smoothing her waist, making her feel sexy in a way she could relish if only she could ignore the urgent hunger in her cunt. She pushed her sex towards him, wanting, wanting. He reached out to her, so slowly she felt she couldn't bear it, and cupped her clamouring cunt in his long dextrous hand. Inhibition lost to all-consuming lust, Sylvie rode his hand vigorously, oblivious to everything except the sensation of the warrior's palm. Usually she liked to feel full, but she didn't have the time to demand penetration, too fixated on the sensations on her clit. The cold water and the firm hand she rubbed against. He laid delicate fingers on her nipple, pushing her over the edge. His strong hand under her mound kept her afloat as she submitted to the hardest orgasm of her life, her pleasure muscles gripping and gripping. As her body juddered its last gorgeous tremor, she was already hungry to be filled. Still held afloat she noticed for the first time that she had an audience.

On the green bank of the pool stood three more men, all as tall and slender as the first and all three of their cocks standing firmly to attention. As one, they entered the water and swam gracefully to her. They encircled her, all looking with fascination at her face and body. Enjoying the attention with a dream's lack of inhibition, Sylvie guessed she must look quite unlikely, otherworldly even, to these people who had probably never seen white skin before. She reached for the nearest erection. Looking right into its owner's eyes, she held it firmly and began to move her hand. The warrior looked helplessly at her from beneath dark brows, his mouth falling slightly open as his breathing increased. His cock was rock hard, with no give whatsoever in its rigid length. She felt it throb at the peak of every stroke and he moved his hips in time with her, fucking her hand. Subconsciously, she moved her opening closer to him, slowing her movements down, but he was unable to reciprocate, compulsively jabbing his hard-on into her hand. The warriors gathered round her, stroking and kissing her skin, their penises rubbing up against her thighs and bum. She felt their hands beneath her and felt her body rise, supported by the men, until she was lying on her back on top of the water. They kissed her front, licking her hard nipples, and the one she was touching moved to bury his face in her sex. Electricity seemed to run through her, from the tongues on her aching nipples to that on her throbbing clit. She thrust into his working mouth, not satisfied, needing to be filled. As if sensing this, the men lowered her bottom back under the water and she felt the spongy head of a penis nosing its way between her folds. She moved, encouraging it, almost crying with desperation for it, until, with a gasp of gratification, the cock found its goal and rode up into her, filling her and nudging at that special area inside her. She felt her orgasm rapidly approaching, each lick and thrust another push toward that perilous edge. But she wasn't ready yet, she wanted to feel like this forever. This was all she wanted, all she needed, she wanted to stop but telling her body to stop fucking was like telling her heart to stop beating. She was locked in the rhythm and it felt like her whole life had led to this moment. Never had sex felt like this. Never had her orgasm had such a life of its own, like a solid, breathing animal, faster than her, more powerful, coming to get her, coming, coming. Every nerve in her body flooded with pleasure, she rocked with the intensity of it, fingers and toes clenching, a primal noise escaping easily from her lips. And the warrior was coming too, holding her tight to him, filling her swallowing cunt with his wild magical sperm. They stayed where they were for a minute, catching their breath, and then one of the not-yet-satisfied warriors demanded his turn. He was perhaps the most handsome of the four, his cheekbones defined and his serious eyes a deeper shade of liquorice. He stared beseechingly into Sylvie's eyes and she kissed him on the mouth, savouring his flavour of fresh herbs and spice. He moved between her legs and slipped into her like the right jigsaw piece. He belonged there. Sylvie felt an intense feeling of warmth and well-being and rocked slowly on his cock, her sensitive part needing little stimulation now. He took his lead from her, and gently circled his hips in a slow and primal dance. This time, she felt climax approaching from far off. It sauntered into view from a distant horizon. The warrior's face was urgent, he didn't need to accelerate his movements, just the feeling of her warm flesh around his swollen cock was enough to make him burst there and then. Sylvie hoped he could hold on until her orgasm was ready. She couldn't be hurried, but the warrior seemed too aroused to wait, too eager to come in her and feast on the pleasure her female body promised. Now she was all he wanted, she was the best that all of life had to offer, sublime pleasure, the cunt of a goddess. He started to come and his throbbing cock pressing its girth against her G-spot tipped her again. Oh YES, she wanted that. She wanted it and he couldn't help but give it to her. She ground herself against his groin, filling herself with every last centimetre of hard flesh. The waves ebbed slowly, and it felt a long time later that she was herself again.

Suddenly, the weight returned to her body as the men turned as one and swam for the rim of the pool. Abandoning all dignity, they scrambled onto the pool edge and knelt low, their faces on the ground towards the sheer stone face of the waterfall, presenting her with a

51

row of muscular buttocks. Sinking low in the water, Sylvie looked up at the source of the falls with apprehension. Her hair swayed around her head like reeds as she waited. She knew she should be afraid, but she couldn't quite feel it; her helplessness to stop what was coming made her feel somehow powerful. A proud body parted the foliage and stood, majestically, at the edge of the cliff. The men flattened themselves minutely lower, but Sylvie's attention was all on their chief.

Standing fully six feet high with dark hair falling free in bountiful waves over her smooth, brown shoulders stood the most beautiful creature Sylvie had ever seen. Her legs were long and powerful, her teeth a brilliant slice of white between succulent lips and the round, ripe fruits of her breasts culminated in nipples that pointed aggressively upward. Her body was naked, but entwined in her hair she wore an organic headdress of leaves and vines. Sylvie's eyes meandered luxuriously down over the chief's defined stomach to the black triangle marking the centre point between her abundant hips. As if presenting herself, the woman turned, showing Sylvie an arse rounder and more shameless than her domestic British eyes were accustomed to. Still, she couldn't hold back a small smile as she imagined sinking her teeth into the plump flesh of those buttocks. As her imagination sent Sylvie's hand sneaking back down beneath the surface of the water, the woman leapt a superhuman leap, her feet clearing her own head and back over to hit the water first. For a long moment she was lost under the glossy surface, then her head rose directly in front of Sylvie, and so close that her hard nipples grazed electric lines up Sylvie's body. Her big mouth opened and took a deep breath before sinking shoulders then head went back under the water. Sylvie felt the mouth clamp onto her wet cunt, sucking out every last vestige of self-control. Every muscle below her waist turned to quivering jelly. The woman's skilful tongue tapped gently on Sylvie's ravaged clit, and she spread her legs wider. The warrior woman took her thighs in her strong hands, tiny bubbles trickling up over her most sensitive part as the woman ate her to the last of her breath. Sylvie heard sounds coming from her own lips and felt her legs shake as if in a dream. The dream seemed to last for hours and days, with nobody but Sylvie and the woman floating, connected mouth and sex, through space. And then she awoke, as the woman burst, gasping, into the air. Still facing Sylvie, she put her arms under her armpits and pushed her backward through the water to bump up against the rough green stone by the waterfall. Pushed up hard against her, the woman brought her face close to Sylvie's, encouraging her to bring her mouth the last inch to meet hers. Watching herself from the outside, Sylvie leant forward and pressed her plump lips onto the even plumper lips of the woman. So soft. So warm. Her tongue reached out tentatively to meet the woman's soft, warm tongue. Sylvie felt she would never settle for a man ever again, a cheap pleasure compared to this soft, engulfing love. She reached out and cupped the woman's breast, lightly at first, and then more firmly as her instincts took over. She leant forward and took the firm nipple between her lips, sucking and teasing the hard teat with her tongue. The woman's hand pushed gently but confidently between Sylvie's legs and she came. Just like that, without warning, a deep warmth spread from her hole and her head lolled back against the wall.

The woman held her, fondling her and kissing lips to neck to chest to lips until she had recovered. Gradually Sylvie began to return the soft feathery kisses on her mouth. It was like returning home. She felt the woman coaxing her along the wall, closer and closer to the waterfall. She started to suspect that they would both be dashed to pieces under the crashing water, but again, failed to feel the fear, giving over all control to the woman. Just as she took the gasp of breath, she found herself not under the fall, but behind it. In a secret cave, three walls stone, one water, the woman rose up to her waist above the surface. The water was colder here and Sylvie ran her fingertips over a Braille of goosebumps from the woman's thigh to her waist. The peak of her breast felt cold under Sylvie's warm lips and she felt the woman's hands at the nape of her neck. Looking up, Sylvie smiled and the woman finally smiled in return. Sylvie's smile broadened, but the woman dropped beneath the surface. Sylvie took a deep breath and followed, back out into the pool. Her head broke the water and she wiped her eyes in time to see the woman and all her followers dissolve into the trees. Straight away she became conscious of a crashing and chattering punctuated by calls of 'SYLVIE??!!'. The familiar sounds brought Joe instantly back into her head, but rather than a painful memory, he seemed like a character in a film she had watched long ago. Here, steeped in ancient sexuality, she realised that what she had had before was nothing but a distraction. The cheap lays and fleeting crushes of her life in Britain held no appeal now. Modern sex, she realised, was nothing but a pale shadow of what the human body was capable of feeling. She turned in the water like a mermaid and dove to the bottom of the pool.

The Butler Did It
by Roger Frank Selby

'Hello?'

'I'm enquiring about the position at Abbey House.'

'Are you phoning on behalf of your husband?'

'No sir; I don't have a husband. *I* am applying for the position.'

He hesitated for a moment. 'I have advertised for the position of a butler; I don't require any other staff at the moment, thank you.'

'I am a butler, sir.'

'Really ...? How extraordinary! Well, I was assuming all butlers were male ... I don't really see how ...'

'Wouldn't you consider a female butler, sir? I'm fully trained, with excellent references.'

'Well, I've never considered it before ... didn't even know there *was* such a thing! And I suppose if I don't grant you an interview I'll be in trouble for being "sexist"!'

'Not for a moment, sir! It is vital that a gentleman is completely comfortable with his butler. Such a thing could never be imposed.' She changed the subject in a businesslike way. 'May I ask how many other staff there are in the household?'

He was warming to her. 'Certainly, Miss ...?'

'Reynolds, sir, just Reynolds.'

'Certainly, Reynolds. Since poor old Forbes passed away we have been getting by with just two, but they are both excellent. Cook, and a maid, Ann ... Look, Reynolds, I guess we could arrange an interview at least. Tuesday all right? Around twelve?'

'Perfect for me, sir.'

'Excellent! Don't forget those references.'

'You'll find I never forget anything. Goodbye, sir.'

'Goodbye, Reynolds.'

The house had a lot of old-fashioned character. A grandfather clock in the hall struck twelve as the maid led the way. A knock, a quiet 'Come', and Reynolds was shown into a roomy, book-strewn study.

'Good afternoon, sir!' He looked a lot younger than she had imagined – probably only just into his forties. He smiled.

'Good afternoon, Reynolds.' He rose to shake hands. He was well built and looked fit – probably still played rugby from time to time by the look of him. 'Would you like a seat?' It was a subtle test.

'No, thank you, sir,' she said, allowing herself a trace of a smile. 'As you know, it would not be appropriate for me to sit down while outside the servants' quarters.'

'Quite right, Forbes – I mean, Reynolds.' My God, she wore a butler's personality so well he'd used his old butler's name ... and yet she was a young woman – hair in a tight bun, and rather heavy spectacles, but unmistakably an attractive woman. Tall and possibly a bit on the skinny side in her grey business suit – slightly padded shoulders. No perfume. She had a strong, intelligent, almost severe face. No make-up. Nice complexion though.

'How old are you, Reynolds?'

'Thirty, sir.'

'Yet you only have three and a half years' experience as a butler. Perhaps you were in service before ...?' He glanced through the two references, scanning swiftly. Sheila Reynolds ... Dazzling words of praise leapt out. Then he found her military discharge papers. 'Ah, a different type of service: an officer in the army!' It explained a lot – her bearing, her presence. 'Why did you leave?'

'It was just a short-service commission, sir.'

'Good, but ... Ah, I'm not sure how quite to put this, Reynolds ...'

'I am unattached, sir.'

Amazing! She could almost read his mind – just like old Forbes. 'Reynolds, I have to say that you are the best candidate by far that I have interviewed. I see from your splendid references that you will have no problem at all running only a couple of staff and this diminutive establishment. The only problem I have is ...'

'Me being a female manservant, sir?'

'Quite.'

'In the past I have started off helping with the ... *less* intimate moments of the day, until my employer was more used to my presence.'

'It's not just that, Reynolds; I'm single, with a wide circle of friends, some of them women. I'm just wondering how they will take to you.'

'I really can't answer that question for you, sir.'

And that's how he started with his new butler. After a few weeks he stopped noticing Reynolds was a woman, so good was she at her job. Occasionally he would go off to the city on business for a few days. Everything seemed to run like clockwork whether he was home or not. Only when he came back late one night with Alison Bradley did he feel the slightest apprehension.

'Oh, it's turned *so* chilly, John!' Alison said as they entered the house. 'I really think it might snow.' Reynolds took Miss Bradley's coat and stole and then her master's coat.

'How was the play, madam?'

'It was marvellous; so clever, Reynolds!' she said archly. 'It turned out that the *butler* did it!'

'Really, madam?'

Alison had a tendency to tease and patronise his people but his butler could take care of herself, thought John. Although Alison had encountered Reynolds a few times before, this was to be the first time his girlfriend would stay overnight. He felt that she might resent Reynolds, might even feel some jealousy towards her … He sensed trouble looming. 'Reynolds, could you get Cook to rustle up some hot chocolate for us?'

'It's all in hand, sir. Cook wasn't feeling too well, so I took the liberty of packing her off to bed early. I put the kettle on when I heard you draw up.'

'Oh, I hope she's not going down with anything,' said Alison, 'John and I were rather looking forward to her eggs and bacon in bed tomorrow morning.'

John cringed but then thought again; good old Forbes would not have batted an eyelid at such a remark.

Neither did Reynolds: 'Don't worry, madam, I can rustle up the best eggs and bacon in the world, just give me ten minutes' notice, day or night!' She turned to her master. 'I'll just put the Aston in the barn while the water's boiling, sir.'

John was sitting with Alison at his feet in front of the drawing room fire when Reynolds brought them their hot chocolate. 'Ah, thank you, Reynolds, that will be all for tonight.'

'Very good, sir. What time will you be wanting breakfast?'

He glanced at Alison. 'About ten OK for you, darling?'

'Yes. Ten o'clock's fine, and make my bacon nice and crispy, please, Reynolds.'

She giggled after Reynolds had closed the door. 'My God, John, she really is *just* like a butler.'

'She *is* a butler, darling, at least the equal of Forbes. Now, come closer.' He slid his hands under the straps of her gown as she leaned back against his knees. Her shoulders were still a little cold. His hands moved lower to cup her pert breasts. They were cool too; deliciously cool.

'Your hands feel so nice and warm on my body, darling,' she whispered. 'I want to make love right here in front of the fire.' She turned her face up to his and he kissed her half-opened mouth.

But what about Reynolds, he thought. Somehow this *wasn't* quite the same as having a male butler. He tried to reason it out. He trusted her. She would not walk in or peep. But somehow, he was not quite so comfortable about sex with Reynolds around. No doubt about it. Could it be because Reynolds was not unattractive herself?

'John! You seem to be miles away.'

'I was just thinking about Reynolds ...' It was out before he could check himself. Honesty was not always the best policy – especially with Alison.

'While you were holding my breasts! Are you comparing them to *her* tits?' She threw off his hands.

He groaned. 'Alison! This is ridiculous! I was doing

59

nothing of the sort. I was just feeling … a little dreamy, thinking about us and my household. Please don't spoil this perfect evening. I'll confess that I *was* worried that she might come in while we were … Anyway,' he tried to laugh it all off, 'Reynolds doesn't appear to have too much in the way of "tits"!'

Alison was not amused. 'John, you are easily taken in. I grant you she looks like a frump, but that is not the case, I know. For some reason she's deliberately hiding her looks and her figure.'

'You know?'

'Yes … Look, John, had you noticed that she and I are about the same age?'

'Well, yes, I had.'

'We were at school together.'

'Good heavens!'

'I didn't mention it before because I didn't want to upset the apple cart. She is a lovely person but something happened to her … I can't say any more. When I first saw her here I wondered if she was gold-digging. But I don't think so now.'

Miss Bradley, worth a few million herself, could never be accused of that. He thought of the possible consequences of this revelation. But as long as both women played the game of not knowing each other, there would be no problem, surely?

At least Alison seems to be back on my side, he thought, kissing her neck and slipping his hands back inside her dress.

They didn't make love by the fire. But they did upstairs: once by the bedroom window, with the curtains open, looking out at the falling snow, once on the carpeted bathroom floor by the mirror and once in his big four-poster bed.

A discreet knock on the door. 'Ten o'clock, sir.'

'Come in, Reynolds,' John called out sleepily.

Alison looked around. The sheet was nowhere in sight in the warm room. She and John were lying naked in each other's arms.

'Good morning, madam, sir. Your breakfast!' Reynolds puffed up the pillows for them both to sit up, the boisterous movement causing her breasts to bounce noticeably beneath her clothing. She found the sheet – which went over their laps – and positioned the tray before them.

'Good morning, Reynolds. You're very kind.'

'My pleasure, madam. Bath in about twenty minutes, sir?'

'Yes, thank you, Reynolds.'

'Did you notice her figure just then?' asked Alison after the door had closed.

'I certainly did! So how well did you know her at school?'

Alison considered her answer for a moment. 'Well, Sheila Reynolds sometimes slept in my bed.'

'Really? Oh, I forgot! Girls can do that sort of thing, without it meaning more than being just friends ...' He must have noticed the quirky smile on her lips. He paused for a moment, 'You and she ...?'

'Yes, John, and it has nothing to do with us. You know how I feel about you.' She touched his arm tenderly. 'I'm only telling you because I don't want us ever to have secrets from each other.'

'You seem very casual about this ... this lesbian thing,' he said, a little sternly.

'I am.'

'Anyone else?'

She took her hand away. 'Not really, it was just her, and only for a while … Look, darling, please don't let us fight about this. I'll be going away soon and I don't want to spoil our precious time together.'

He was very thoughtful as he munched on his toast. He was still quiet as they lay in the big bath at opposite ends, with none of their usual hanky-panky.

Damn! Perhaps she'd been a fool to be so honest. She really didn't want to lose him – and she might have jeopardised Sheila's career. 'Sheila is no more a complete lesbian than I am, John. But this "butler" thing is something else. She had a terrible experience in the Gulf, you know. I think it has permanently scarred her.'

'Combat duty?'

'She was raped by a gang of soldiers … on *our* side.'

His mouth dropped open and the bathwater surged as he sat up straight. 'Good Lord!'

'She asked me not to tell *anyone* – you in particular.'

'So you *have* been talking?'

'Just catching up a little, darling.'

John could be a little insensitive sometimes, but he had a very kind heart. 'My God! The poor girl … Maybe that's why … it's almost as if she doesn't want to be a woman any more.'

'She has an underlying fear of men. I guess the formal butler persona allows her to handle things better. She has a bad case of penile phobia, apparently … Oops! Promise me you'll never tell her I told you any of this?'

'Good Lord … darling, my lips are sealed.' He leaned forward with a splash and kissed her. They seemed to be right back to normal.

He pulled the cord.

'Sir?'

'The hot towels, please, Reynolds. Miss Bradley can

go first.'

Reynolds held open the vast towel. Alison stepped out and turned to face John as Reynolds dried her back and legs. In the heat Reynolds was working without her jacket and Alison had already noticed that the butler wasn't wearing a bra under her blouse.

John must have noticed too. Alison opened her eyes wide when she saw the monster rising out from the bathwatery depths.

Despite his state of arousal he was a perfect gentleman as always. 'Reynolds, thank you ... We will be fine ...'

'No.' Alison was as firm as her boyfriend was becoming. 'It's all right for Reynolds to stay. Your turn next, darling.'

John shrugged his shoulders and grinned. 'Me next, then, Reynolds, if that's all right with you.'

'It's perfectly fine with me, sir.'

He stood up and stepped out of the bath, as erect as a man can be. Reynolds stared at him, her mouth slightly open.

Well, if Sheila still has penile phobia, this is the moment of truth, thought Alison. She watched, enthralled, while John's back and legs were vigorously towelled, as if he were a stallion being rubbed down in the stables. She saw the beautiful feminine motion of Sheila's half-hidden breasts in time with John's manly swing. She became more aroused than she had ever been in her life. When she spoke, her voice was thick with desire. 'Let me lend a hand there, Sheila.' She dropped her covering towel and fell naked to her knees before him. Grabbing a small hand towel she started to dry every inch of the man. Sheila watched the kneeling woman at her task. 'Come down here,' said Alison. 'I'll show you how to dry him thoroughly.'

'Are you sure, madam?'

'I'm quite sure.' Sheila slowly knelt down beside her. Alison pushed another small towel into her hand. 'It's very important to make sure he's dry here behind his balls, right at the root of his cock. Open your legs a little please, darling. That's right, Sheila, lift them gently and dry behind. There, see what I mean?'

John felt the towel and the light touch of female fingers, saw his cock reaching out over the kneeling women.

'Yes ... that is perfectly clear, madam.'

'Call me "Alison" for a while, Sheila. Let us *all* call each other by our first names. And please let me help you out of that hot blouse.'

He saw Sheila's arms lift as she pulled off the blouse herself; saw her perfect breasts moving freely.

'Now don't you say a word, John. I want to show you off to my good friend Sheila. Now, Sheila, hold on to his cock with both of your hands.'

Sheila reached out, touching him very lightly at first, then holding him with growing confidence. He revelled in her touch as she gripped him more firmly.

'Now, Sheila, I want to show *you* off to my male lover, John. You have been hiding the most beautiful pair of tits a woman can have. I want you to let my lover touch them.' He needed no further encouragement. He leaned forward, filling his hands. He felt the yielding weight of the breasts of the kneeling woman; let his thumbs feel the darker, up-standing tips. He could see the reflection of him fondling her body in the bathroom mirror.

'Do you feel him reacting to your lovely body, Sheila? Feel how hard he is, how hot he is. Press his cock hard against your cheek.'

Alison watched Sheila looking at her own reflection, that of a half-nude woman being intimately fondled and squeezed by big male hands while she held on to his cock. This must be her first time since that horrific experience.

Sheila was hesitating, a panicky look in her eyes. She let go. Alison acted immediately: 'John, quick! Get down on your back, close your eyes ... We just need your dick on his own for a while, darling.'

He did as he was told.

'There is nothing to be frightened about, Sheila,' she said, stroking her friend's breasts where John had been forced to let go. 'This dangerous-looking weapon is more under *our* control than his. Let me show you.'

John kept his eyes screwed tightly closed as he felt the handling fingers of both women making his cock react. He recognised Sheila's grip return more firmly than before. Only when he felt the brush of long hair on his belly did he take a peek.

Sheila had let her hair down.

As she lowered her mouth he felt her deep breasts make contact with his opened thighs. He also felt the gentle spurt of a little pre-fluid.

'Oops, don't worry, Sheila, I'll lick that one off for you ...'

The familiar tongue.

'Lovely,' said Alison. 'You try the next one. There'll be a lot more where that came from. While you're doing that I'll undo your skirt. There. You have such lovely long legs, Sheila.'

He felt Sheila's wet mouth come fully down over his

cockhead for the first time. It was warm and soft. He felt the texture of her tongue lick along his shaft ... Oops! Another spurt. He'd felt it coming and managed to control it. She gagged a little but held on.

'And now I'll just slide these panties off your lovely bottom ... and right down ... and kick them off!' continued Alison. 'Such a lovely bottom ... that's right; keep it high so I can feel all around, over and under where you are so wet ... I will just touch you where we women love to be touched ...'

He felt Sheila's teeth as her head jumped. He couldn't help letting out a yelp.

'Nipped him a little, eh? Have to remember to keep your mouth well open; but it gives you a sense of power and control, doesn't it? And remember, he is trusting you with the most important thing in his life ... I'll continue to stroke your tits and play with you while you suck him. That's it, roll your bottom around, girl. Roll it around my fingers. I'll slip my fingers up into you like this ... You are so tight and wet ... Any time you want to pull off my hand and sit on my lover, feel free, but don't wait too long or *I'll* have him! He'll be coming soon. Do you want to try him, Sheila?'

John opened his eyes and saw Sheila lift her mouth just clear of the glistening head of his cock. She looked sideways at her love-friend with half-closed eyes. A filament of fluid still joined her lips to him. 'Yes, Alison,' she breathed, 'I think I'm ready now.'

'Then stand astride your man facing his feet.' She did, and John saw that she had the most beautiful bottom. 'Now squat down slowly and I'll guide you. Almost there ... There! Feel him, just splitting you? He's in perfect position; any time you want to take him in, just squat right down. Take as little, or as much as you want. You are in complete control. And there … I can still play with you, you're wide open; and *so* wet …'

Sheila lowered her head and groaned as Alison's fingers moved against her clitoris. Slowly she squatted down. She moaned as John felt his broad cockhead make deeper contact, spread her a little and then slide right in. She gasped, then squatted down further; trying it ever deeper inside her.

John raised his hands and held the cheeks of her buttocks. She slowly sat right down. All the way. Deep inside he felt her cervix brush the sensitive tip of his cock.

'That's it, Sheila! He is right up inside you. But be careful, come down too quickly and too far and it will hurt.'

She was tight but very slippery on him. He was about to explode into her. He tried to relax. He partly succeeded, just delivering a gentle spurt. It eased and smoothed the motion as she began to bob gently up and down on him, trying longer and longer strokes.

'Doesn't that feel good, Sheila?'

'Ahhhh, yes,' she moaned, 'And please don't stop … what *you're* doing … Uhhhh …'

'I won't! We'll keep on like this, up and down, rolling around, up and down until I make you …'

John cried out.

He could hold back the tide no longer. He began to release, shooting up, spurting his seed into the woman in long rushes.

'Ah, there we are … John, my love, let her have it, let it all go, fill her up! That's it, Sheila, keep riding him, get your head down and watch him pumping into you. That's it, girl, you can howl your heart out. John, keep coming … Fill her up with your sperm … Fuck her well.

When you're done I want to see it running down Sheila's thighs, flowing everywhere, just like when you've fucked me.'

The taxi arrived. It was time for Alison to leave.

'Are you sure I can't drive you there, darling?'

'I won't hear of it.' She kissed him. 'I hate long goodbyes at the airport. And you ... *Sheila*.' With a sob Alison hugged her. They kissed. As they separated John saw that both women were openly weeping.

He and Reynolds waved as the departing taxi retraced its tracks on the snow-covered drive.

'May I speak to you freely for a moment, sir? While we are outside the house.'

'Certainly, Reynolds, what's on your mind? But make it quick; it's cold!' He attempted a smile. He guessed what was on her mind.

'I'm afraid I must reluctantly give you my notice.'

He was silent for a moment. 'Damn! I was afraid this might happen after that ... *madness* this morning. That *wonderful* madness ... I'm so sorry if ...'

'Don't be sorry, *John*; if I can say your name just once. It *was* wonderful. The two of you ... And I was more than willing. But it's changed everything. I just can't carry on here in this position.'

'Are you absolutely sure?'

'Absolutely. I would like to go *immediately*, sir, if possible. I know that a week's notice is the normal minimum, and I'll work a week if you insist, but Cook and Ann are here and able to look after you.'

Ann and Mrs Marcos were there with him to see her off. A handshake, a few empty words of farewell, then her car too was making its dark tracks down the drive as the snow began to drift down again.

The next few days passed miserably. He neglected his work, apart from advertising the post of a gentleman's gentleman – sexist, perhaps – but it made clear the requirement beyond all doubt.

A knock on the study door.

'Come.'

'Lady to see you, sir, about the housekeeper's job.'

'Yes, OK, Ann … But I haven't advertised for a …' A shapely woman with long brown hair was standing just behind her. 'Reynolds!' He sprang to his feet. 'You look fantastic!'

She walked in with a natural sway of her hips, wearing a smart dress that didn't hide the curves of her body.

'Call me Sheila, please, sir! I'm no longer a butler. I'm a *housekeeper*. I thought you might like to try a housekeeper instead of a butler for a while.'

'*Sheila*.' He savoured the name. 'I can call you that as housekeeper!'

'It's the first time you have called me that.'

'Even when …?'

'Even then!'

Dream Lover
by Elizabeth Cage

I've always loved velvet. It's so soft and sensual, perfect for an erotic encounter. My wardrobe is full of velvet skirts and dresses. I can choose from mysterious black, deep, rich burgundy, wine-bottle green. Or blue. Midnight blue is my favourite. For me, velvet is the most romantic of fabrics. It looks great and feels wonderful. I like to be stroked when I'm wearing velvet – it makes me purr like a cat. Kind of a fetishy thing, I suppose. Just thinking about it makes me tremble. In fact, I'd just bought a new black velvet coat, trimmed with fake fur, when I met Perry.

It was a Friday night and I was sitting in a crowded wine bar with my friend, Amy, celebrating my recent redundancy with copious amounts of gin and tonic.

'Don't you think it's a tiny bit irresponsible to be splashing out on a new coat when you were told less than four hours ago that you were out of a job?' suggested Amy tentatively.

'Bugger responsible,' I retorted, taking another swig from my glass. 'I'm sick of nine to five, sick of being told what to do. It's time I had some fun, took a few chances.'

'But you won't have any dosh to have fun with, once

'your redundancy money is gone,' she pointed out.

'There is that, I suppose,' I shrugged. 'But I'll always have my lovely little collection of credit cards. Thank God for plastic, I say.'

Amy sighed and I could see she'd decided to give up on me for the time being. Security has always been important to Amy. She's been settled down and married to Bill, her childhood sweetheart, for six years now, with two bouncing little sprogs to show for it. Which is why she wasn't joining me on the G&Ts. She was doing the driving tonight.

'I'd better not stay much longer,' she said, anxiously glancing at her watch. 'I promised Bill I'd be home by seven.'

'Bugger Bill. Live a little,' I muttered, raising my glass in a gesture of defiance.

'It's not that simple,' she replied. 'I have to get back to look after the kids so Bill can go to his evening class.'

'Right. Domestic bliss and all that. Let you out for the party tomorrow, will he?'

'Of course. We *are* two separate people, you know. We're not joined at the hip. Besides, being part of a couple can be –'

'Wonderful,' I grunted. 'That's a matter of opinion.'

'You haven't met the right bloke, that's all,' she continued doggedly. 'You might meet someone at the party.'

'Hmm. After the last man I dated, I'm not sure if I want to.' And I recalled the appropriately named Dick who sent me flowers every Monday and professed his undying love for me while he screwed around behind my back with other women. I came home early from work one day to discover him rogering a gorgeous-looking brunette with twice the energy he'd ever put into our lovemaking. But what really pissed me off was that she was having what sounded like the biggest orgasm in the history of the universe.

'Don't forget it's a fancy dress party,' Amy reminded me, jolting me back to the present. 'Vicars and tarts. So just wear your usual gear.'

'Ha! Very original, Amy. You do, of course, mean my clerical gown and dog collar?'

'Obviously.' Giggling, she said, 'Can I borrow your leather miniskirt? I don't have anything remotely tarty to wear and –'

'I have a whole wardrobe to choose from. All right. Come round in the morning and have a rummage. I'll pay for these drinks. My treat.'

I reached for my handbag. For some reason, it wasn't hanging over my chair where I'd left it. Nor was it lurking beneath the table.

'Amy,' I said, trying not to panic, 'I think someone's stolen my bag.'

The guy running the wine bar was very kind, letting me use the phone there to call the bank and credit card company.

'I hate to leave you like this, Naomi, but I really have to get home,' apologised Amy, getting agitated. 'Bill will be late for his bookkeeping class as it is.'

'I'll be fine,' I replied, not feeling fine at all. In fact, when she'd gone, I almost burst into tears.

'Don't worry, Naomi.' The wine bar guy was standing beside me. 'I'm sure everything will be all right.' His voice was soft and comforting. And sexy.

He smiled, showing neat white teeth. 'I'm Perry. Why don't you stay here and have another drink? On the house.'

I accepted gratefully. 'You know, Perry, I lost my job

72

today.'

'That's terrible,' he said sympathetically.

'I ask you, how unlucky can a girl get in one day?'

He took my hand and smiled warmly. 'Don't worry, Naomi, however bad it seems, I think the fates have a way of sorting things out for the better.'

'Really? You believe that?'

'Really. Now, would you like me to top your glass up?'

Perry stayed close by for the rest of the evening, assigning other staff to look after the customers while he took care of me. I was flattered, and hardly aware that people were drifting away as it got nearer to closing time.

'Perhaps I should call you a taxi,' he offered. 'Will you be OK? I mean, won't your boyfriend be worrying?'

'Boyfriend. Ha!' I growled sarcastically. 'Don't believe in boyfriends. Only good for one thing and not even that.'

'I see,' he said, smiling benignly.

'Well, at least I've still got my coat,' I slurred, cuddling it protectively. 'Would you like to see it?'

And I slipped it over my shoulders and pouted in what I imagined was a seductive manner.

'It's a very lovely coat, Naomi,' he agreed. 'Black velvet. May I touch it?'

And before I could reply, Perry ran his fingers lightly down my arm, and I felt an unexpected tingle of electricity.

'Beautiful,' he breathed. 'Such a sensuous fabric.'

I shuddered. 'Do that again,' I said.

Gently, Perry placed his hands on my shoulders and slowly, carefully, caressed me through the coat – along my elbows, down to my wrists and then lingering on my

73

hands. Finally, he bent his head to my fingertips, kissing each one. Trembling, I muttered, breathing hard, 'Again.'

This time, Perry deftly wrapped his hands around my waist and lifted me onto the empty bar in one swift movement.

'I love your coat, Naomi,' he murmured, pulling it open and running his hands down my stockinged legs, letting my black high heels drop to the floor with a soft thud. 'You know what? I think it would look *soooo* much better if you were naked beneath it.'

My head was spinning from a mixture of alcohol and sexual excitement. You don't know this man, a tiny voice inside my head warned me. Who cares? answered the flaming heat between my thighs.

'Take off your dress, Naomi.'

How could I resist that voice? Oblivious to the fact that we were probably providing a free show for any passers-by, I slipped off the velvet coat and wriggled out of the figure-hugging red dress that Amy had frequently told me was too sexy to wear for the office – particularly when I didn't have a bra on. Like today, for instance.

Perry's eyes widened when he saw my firm white breasts, the nipples already hard, and as he leaned forward to wrap my coat around me, the bulge in his black jeans was unmistakable. While he longingly kissed the nape of my neck, Perry took my narrow waist in his broad hands, slowly sliding them down to my hips until they found my black lace suspender belt. Gently but firmly, he unclipped it, dropping it to the floor, along with my flimsy black silk knickers. Running his hands down my seamed stockings, he unpeeled first one, then the other, tenderly kissing each anklebone in turn. The tip of his tongue probed between each toe and I trembled, longing for that tongue to explore my aching pussy.

'You're very wet, Naomi,' he observed. 'I think perhaps that pretty cunt of yours needs some attention.' And he plunged his head between my thighs while I cried out with pleasure. He took complete control, his tongue flicking lightly, barely a whisper of whisky breath on my clitoris. Then, when the sensations became unbearably delicious, he increased the pressure, little by little, until the first wave crashed over me and I was coming, my body arcing violently. Still he continued, licking and sucking, taking my throbbing flesh between his teeth, nibbling, teasing, and my body was once more wracked with currents of exquisite pleasure. After my third orgasm, Perry stopped, and said quietly, 'Do you feel better now, Naomi?'

'Hmm,' I groaned hungrily, reaching for the zip on his jeans. 'But I want you inside me, Perry. Now.'

'Not tonight, Naomi,' he replied, smiling. 'I never fuck on the first date. It's bad manners, don't you think?' Noting my surprise and disappointment, he added quickly, 'What about tomorrow?'

To cut a long story short, Perry and I dated every night that week. Correction. We made love every night. Frequently. Ravenously. It was as if I'd been on a diet but had just been given permission to gorge myself on all the chocolate I could cram into my mouth. Perry was as good with his cock as he was with his tongue. And he was pretty damn talented with his fingers, too. In fact, if anyone had asked me to rate them in order of skill, I would have been hard-pressed to make a decision.

'I'm sorry I didn't make the party,' I told Amy over coffee at my place one morning. 'I met this guy. We've been seeing rather a lot of each other, so to speak.'

'Sounds fun,' Amy grinned. 'So where did you meet him?'

'The wine bar. Last week.'

'What's he like, then? Handsome, charming, great lover ...'

I nodded. 'All of those. Actually, you met him there, too.'

She frowned. 'I did?'

'Remember the wine bar owner?'

'I'm impressed! You don't waste any time, Naomi,' she joked.

'Neither does he,' I laughed. 'He's amazing. In every way. Amy, I'm sure I've found the man of my dreams.'

Perry was more than a great lover. He seemed interested in everything about me. He noticed what I wore, and often commented on it. This was quite a novelty, since my previous boyfriends were philistines in this area; once the initial novelty had worn off of snaring a new female, I was lucky if I raised a grunt from them if I asked for an opinion on my latest outfit. Perry, however, even bought me clothes – gorgeous, expensive dresses and skirts – in sumptuous fabrics. Particularly velvet. He suggested that I try out different styles and colours, paying attention to the cut and weight of the fabric. It was a long time since I had been the object of such undivided attention. And I loved every minute of it. In fact, I even let him persuade me to change the hairstyle I'd kept since my teens.

'I know a wonderful hairdresser,' he kept telling me. 'Or should I say, hair designer. He can make you look even more stunning.'

'Don't you like blonde hair?' I asked him, surprised. Most of the guys I knew before Perry went for blondes in a big way.

'Of course,' he replied. 'But I think that black looks so much more dramatic. Mysterious. Sexy.'

'Oh.' I hesitated. I'd never coloured my hair before. I liked the fact I was a natural blonde. 'Don't you think going black might be a bit radical?'

'Trust me,' he replied in that dark velvety voice of his.

So my waist-length tresses were cut and dyed into a stylish black close crop. Perry was delighted with my new look. I wasn't so sure. It was a bit of a shock, seeing my lovely blonde hair being swept off the salon floor and tossed into the bin. But Perry insisted the transformation was everything he had imagined.

'Perfect,' he whispered into my ear as he wrote out the rather large cheque. 'Simply perfect.' And his lips brushed over my now exposed neck, sending tremors down my spine that seemed to culminate in my clit.

But as time went on, I realised that his efforts to change me were perhaps a bit over the top. I didn't notice at first, because he was subtle, dropping small hints.

'Don't you think that skirt's a bit short? Not that it doesn't look good, of course, and I like short skirts, but I think a longer length in that particular style suits your figure better. And what about trying this colour lipstick instead of your usual shade?'

I began to wonder what was behind this. Was he going off me?

'Perry, do you still find me attractive?' I asked one night after a bout of passionate sex.

'Why, darling,' he replied looking hurt. 'You know I think you are the sexiest, most beautiful woman on earth.' He planted a series of butterfly kisses around the base of my spine as I lay face down on black satin

77

sheets. I had to stop myself from melting, but I was determined to pursue this.

'Have you ever been married before?' I continued.

'No, never,' he said looking up at me. 'I promise that you're the woman of my dreams.'

'Really?'

'*Really*.' He slid his sensitive fingers between my legs. 'Satisfied?'

'Hmmmmm. That feels good.'

'You want more?'

'Much more.'

'Well, you asked for it.'

He rolled over on top of me, his swollen cock resting on my belly, and I clamped my hands around it, anticipating how it would feel when it filled and stretched me.

'Turn over,' and he flipped me onto my back. 'Lift up your hips.' Within seconds he was pushing into my gaping cunt, thrusting energetically until I was gasping for breath, then slowing down until he had almost stopped, making me wait, bringing me repeatedly to the edge until finally, unable to hold back any longer, we exploded together.

Afterwards, when I was nestled in his protective arms, thinking how lucky I was to have found such a considerate lover, he said casually, 'By the way, there's someone I want you to meet tomorrow night.'

'Who?'

'It's a surprise.'

I spent the next day trying to figure out who it could be. His boss? A gorgeous twin brother? I rather liked this idea and found myself imagining what it might be like to be made love to by two Perrys.

By the time I was ready to see him, I was trembling

with anticipation, having geared myself up to the thought of a mind-blowing threesome. I opened the car door and stepped out carefully, smoothing my dress down. It was Perry's favourite, and he had specially requested that I wear it tonight. Made of stretchy blue velvet, it moulded to my hips and thighs. It was short. Very short. I was also wearing my black shiny shoes with six-inch heels, which made my bare legs look even longer and my dress even shorter. I wasn't wearing any knickers so when I bent over the seat to reach for my handbag, little was left to the imagination. Taking a deep breath I straightened up and walked purposefully up the drive, tottering a little in the heels.

As arranged, I arrived at his flat at 7.30 p.m., breathing in the smell of his excellent cooking as soon as he opened the door. (This man could cook nearly as well as he could fuck.)

'Hello, darling.' He kissed my forehead.

'So, who am I going to meet?' I asked impatiently.

He gave a secretive smile and for some reason, I began to feel uneasy. As I stepped into the lounge I smelt a familiar perfume – just like the one Perry had bought for my birthday. Surely it wasn't an ex-girlfriend? Or perhaps my dream lover was married after all …

'She's in the bathroom,' said Perry. 'She'll be out in a minute. I can't wait for the two of you to meet.'

He'd just finished speaking when the 'she' in question came out and we met face to face. We could have been identical twins, except she was about twenty years older than me. It was uncanny. She was wearing the same dress, in sky blue velvet, and her hair was the same dark crop cut. But it got worse.

'Naomi. I want you to meet my mother,' Perry

announced proudly.

In my haste to leave, I almost picked up the wrong coat, which was hardly surprising because Perry's mother also had a velvet coat with fur trimmings – very similar to mine, in fact.

A policeman turned up last night to say my handbag had been handed in (empty, of course).

'Never let your handbag or purse out of your sight in future,' he advised in his deep, slightly gravelly voice. 'There are too many professional thieves operating round here.' As he spoke, I thought how smart he looked in his uniform, with perfectly pressed trousers and polished buttons and all manner of shiny things that dangled and jangled from his leather belt. His handcuffs looked particularly eye-catching. Even his helmet, which nestled beside him on the sofa, was impressive. Noble, somehow. A symbol of authority.

He didn't seem in a hurry to go, and I joked that there clearly wasn't much crime on his patch for him to be able to spend his time chatting to me.

We're going to see a film together on Saturday night. An erotic thriller. It's had good reviews – supposed to be quite sexy. I'm meeting him at the cinema, straight after his shift finishes. But I've told him to keep his uniform on – particularly the leather belt with shiny attachments. I have a new fetish now, you see.

Last Night
by Dakota Rebel

Lying in bed together, talking to each other in those last few minutes before sleep pulled us apart, that was the best part of every day. I loved to be wrapped in his arms with my head on his chest, listening to the low rumble as he talked about his day. My fingers would always wind around the short hairs on his chest while he spoke. I would linger over his heart because I loved the feel of it beating against our skin.

Last night was no different. He pulled me against him before my second leg had even swung up on to the bed. I had missed him too. He had just come home from a business trip that had lasted entirely too long. We had talked on the phone every night he was gone, but it was a poor substitute for the feel of his skin against mine. After six years together even one night apart was an eternity. But he was home and there would be no more nights of a cold, empty bed to crawl into for a long time.

I don't know if it was our jobs, the cold weather that had moved into the area recently or if we just craved the closeness that only being snuggled under the blankets together could give us. But it was only about 11 p.m., and he was exhausted. I felt pretty tired too because I never slept well when he was away. We had been going to bed earlier lately as it was, and the added stress of his trip seemed to have drained both of us even more than usual.

I wrapped my arm over his chest to take my usual place while he told me about what he had done on his trip. I cracked jokes and made him laugh, the sound low and deep against my ear on his chest. My love for him was always strong, but at night, when it was just us in bed, I felt it even more. Those small moments out of our hectic days let me know that we could survive anything. We joked that we were too polite to ever divorce, but that was never really it. It was our ability to share, to touch and to love without remorse that would ensure our future together. I loved this man more than I could have ever imagined.

He leaned down to kiss me goodnight, a gentle press of lips before he would turn away to sleep. But last night, I wanted a real kiss. He had been away from me too long for me to accept anything gentle. Every night he had been gone I had imagined what I wanted to do to him when he was finally with me again and I was not about to let him get away that easily.

I snaked my hand around the back of his neck, pulling him tighter against me. I parted his lips with my tongue and he chased my tongue back into my mouth with his own. He licked across my lips, gently sucking the bottom one into his warm, wet mouth. I groaned softly at the feel of it which made him smile.

He rolled me on top of him, his fingers tangled in my hair, his palms caressing the back of my jaw. I straddled his hips with my thighs while I continued to kiss him deeply, our tongues and our teeth crashing violently against one another. He tasted so fucking good. He always did, like toothpaste and a deeper, more earthy taste under that, that taste that was all him. Better than any candy I had ever eaten.

I pulled myself away from his mouth to kiss a wet trail down the side of his throat then back up to his earlobe. He used to have earrings, little gold hoops in both ears. God how I loved the way they clacked loudly against my teeth, the way the sound of it made him moan. But his work obligations dictated that he lose them. So now I had to be careful not to bite too hard because there was not metal to protect his lobe from my teeth any more. Sometimes I forgot. And sometimes I didn't, but bit too hard anyway.

He shifted beneath me, his arousal obvious against my pyjama-clad body. I scooted my ass up slightly, rubbing against his erection and being rewarded for the movement with a deep growl from his throat. I kissed him again, my tongue practically fucking his mouth. He wrapped his arms around me, pulling me closer so he could roll over and lie on top of me, positioning his lower half between my legs. I responded by rubbing myself against his bulging cock. The friction between us was driving me mad and I loved it. He felt amazing. I wanted him inside me even though I knew I shouldn't. So we kissed and touched and dry humped like teenagers in their parents' basement on a Saturday night.

There were certain times every month when I was not comfortable making love, and I had warned him that it was going to be one of those times. These were always the days we chose to act sexually wanton toward each other. It had become sort of a game to see who could drive the other more insane with desire. He knew when the make-out session began that we were not going to have sex, but he never once asked me to stop. He accepted and gave back as good as he got with the torture. Rubbing against me any time I stopped rubbing on him, making me want him more and more with every touch.

It had been a long couple of days. I could tell he was enjoying himself, but his eyes had closed to slits somewhere between sleep and arousal. Our kissing slowed in tempo then reduced itself to light pecks and soft caresses. He slid off of me and we lay next to each other with our fingers entwined for a few minutes.

When we had both calmed ourselves, slightly, we resumed our sleeping positions. He kissed me gently on the lips then rolled over, the curve of his tight little ass wedged against my stomach. I fluttered butterfly kisses over his shoulder, making him groan. I wrapped my arm over him, gently stroking his chest hair with my fingers. He may have been tired again, but I was wide awake. I let my hand travel down his chest and over his stomach. I played a finger along the inside of the elastic band of his boxers then slowly slid my hand down, caressing the top of his thigh.

He stayed perfectly still, not saying a word, either to stop or to encourage me. But his breathing gradually sped up again and I knew what he was expecting me to do. I ran my fingers lightly over his cock, barely a whisper of a touch from the base to his tip. I swirled my finger around the pre-cum that was pooling at his crown, withdrawing my hand to noisily suck my finger clean by his ear. He still remained silent, but his ass was pushing harder against me and I could see his teeth biting into the corner of his lip.

I moved my hand back into his boxers and gripped his cock hard in my hand. I started slowly pumping him until his hips started moving in rhythm with my hand, then I moved faster. He moaned softly, the small noise emboldening me further. I moved my face so that I could breathe on his ear and he shuddered for me.

'Do you want me to suck your cock?' I whispered.

'Yes. God, please yes,' he panted, grabbing my wrist to pull my hand away from his pulsing erection.

'Then tell me.'

'Please suck my dick.'

'Don't ask me, fucking tell me.' My mouth was pressed against his ear and I growled the words at him.

'Suck my cock!'

I smiled down at him for a moment. I loved that only I had the power to get him in that kind of state. His eyes were wide open again, his chest heaving as he kicked his legs out of his boxers. He lay there naked, erect, waiting for me to do as I was told. But he knew telling me to suck him off had only been at my request, so he was not in control of how I would do it. I was in control, I would set the pace, I would do as I wanted to him, and he would come when I was ready for him to come.

I slid down so I could put my mouth softly around the tip of his cock. He moved as if he would reach for my head, but then he dropped his hands to the bed by his hips.

'Good boy,' I whispered.

Any thought of sleeping we may have had was gone. I was aching to taste him, to tease him, to make him hurt until he begged me to let him come. I licked my lips then took the smooth head of his cock into my mouth again, swirling my tongue around it as if it were the sweetest ice cream cone I had ever tasted. I slid down his shaft and when my forehead touched his stomach I lay there, still as I could, letting him feel my throat convulse around the head of his cock buried deep inside me. He pulled back before I did; he always did when I deep-

85

throated him like that. He would never tell me if it was because I was hurting him, or he was afraid of hurting me. He moved his hand around my chin and fondled his balls. I violently pushed his hand away and he moaned again.

'Mine,' I said firmly. I wrapped my right hand around the base of his cock, pumping slowly up and down. My left hand slid between his legs so I could press lightly on the tight ring of muscles at his anus. He shifted his legs to give me better access to anything I wanted to touch. I smiled up at him for a moment before putting my lips around his cock again.

I moved my hand in time with my mouth to keep from choking while I concentrated on slowly probing his asshole with my finger. When I had the first finger all the way in I slowly inserted a second, moving them back and forth to work the muscles loose so I didn't hurt him.

He cried out at the sensations, his hands finally reaching for my head to try and slow me down. But I didn't want to slow down. I wanted to feel him, taste him, make him scream for me. I moved my right hand, smacking at his arms to get him to move. He did, reluctantly.

I fucked him with my mouth as fast as I could, his cock hitting the back of my throat forcefully. His hands clenched in the sheets, so I knew he was close to coming for me.

I crooked the fingers inside of his ass, pressing hard against that small, sweet spot inside of him. He screamed, scratching at the wall next to us as his scent hit my nostrils with a taste like liquid sugar and oysters flooding my mouth, sliding over my tongue. I pulled out my fingers so I could gently massage his balls while he pumped his seed down my throat.

I let him slip from between my lips then placed a light kiss on his thigh, causing him to squirm and laugh quietly. I climbed up his body and he placed a soft kiss on my lips.

'I love you,' I said, snuggling against him, my fingers playing in the fine hair on his chest.

'I love you too.'

'Can I do that again?' I asked.

'I don't think I could take you doing that again right now. Maybe you should wake me up in the middle of the night.' He had said it as if it were a joke, but I thought it was a great idea.

'Goodnight,' he said. He kissed my forehead before turning over to sleep.

'Goodnight, sweetie.' I lay in the dark, listening to his breathing even out, rolling on to my side when I knew he was asleep. I looked over at the clock to see that it was almost midnight. I grabbed the alarm so I could set it for 3 a.m. I figured that would be plenty of sleep for him before I did it again.

I smiled to myself as I closed my eyes. It was so good to have him home.

Sacrifice
by Jim Baker

'Trick or treat!'

I peered at the small faces through a whisky haze, threw some sweets towards them and slammed the apartment door.

I picked up the bottle.

God – four years to the day since it happened. How I wish we had never been to look at that house.

'What's that?'

Joanne was peering out of the window into the misty garden.

'What, love?'

'Down there on the lawn. That hut thing.'

'That's the summerhouse, madam.' The estate agent joined us by the window. 'Very sought after.'

'Sought after? That thing?'

'Well, you can't see it properly from here,' the agent said testily. 'I'm sure your children will love it.'

Joanne smiled at him.

'Our daughter's nearly seventeen. I'm not sure a summerhouse will be her thing. But we'll take a look.'

We left the agent in the house and walked across the lawn to the small wooden building. It was dark coloured and dirty and, as we went inside, I had the feeling of invading something. Something, or someone, very old. The door swung partly closed and the light faded.

I turned to my wife. 'It's not much of a place …' I stopped in surprise at the expression on her face. Her eyes were closed and she seemed to be listening intently.

'What is it?'

Her eyes snapped open, and blood rushed to her face. Her whole body shuddered and she gasped as if in pain.

I moved quickly across and she collapsed into my arms.

'What is it, Jo? What's wrong?'

She clung to me, breathing hard, and then pushed herself upright.

'I came,' she whispered. Her face was still blood red.

'What?'

'I came. I just had a fantastic orgasm.'

I stared at her.

'An orgasm? But how? I mean …'

She shook her head, slowly, and looked unseeingly at me.

'I don't know. There was the chanting and then I was coming so hard I … but something …'

She stopped and shivered. The gloom intensified and the dank wooden hut seemed to shrink around us.

'Come on,' I said. 'Let's get out of here.' I took her hand and moved towards the door. For a moment she resisted, then followed me outside, where pale sunshine was beginning to disperse the morning mist.

We walked back to the house, where the agent was still waiting, in silence.

'Well, what did you think of the summerhouse?' he enquired hopefully.

'I didn't …' I began but got no further.

'It's lovely!'

Joanne smiled brightly at the somewhat surprised man. 'And you're right – our daughter will love it. We'll be in touch with you very soon to make an offer on the house. Come on, darling.'

She took my hand and pulled me towards the door.

We walked to the car in silence and got in. I turned to her.

'That was a bit sudden, wasn't it? I mean, I know we agreed we like the place, but it is the first one we've really looked at …'

She smiled dreamily at me.

'It's perfect, darling. You'll see.'

I looked closely at her.

'Jo, are you OK? What happened in the summerhouse? What did you hear?'

An odd, sly expression flickered across her face and was gone. She moved closer to me.

'Just some singing, darling. I expect I imagined it.'

She moved her hand on to my knee.

'Don't start the engine yet. Wait until he's gone.'

She nodded through the side window towards the agent, who was getting into his car. He waved as he drove past us up the driveway and out of sight.

Joanne's hand was on my crotch now, and her fingers were playing with my cock through my pants.

'Jo …'

'Hush, baby. Relax. It's your turn.'

Her voice was hypnotic and my cock was getting hard.

I felt my pants being unbuttoned and unzipped and then cool fingertips stroked my hot flesh and I groaned softly. I sagged back in the seat and closed my eyes.

'He's so hard, baby. So very hard. And I'm so horny.'

Her breath tickled my ear, and her perfume made my head swim. Soft lips kissed the tip of my cock, and very slowly moved down the shaft until it was deep in her throat. Some misgiving stirred inside me, and vanished as she began to suck.

Lips, fingers and tongue combined to build me to a slow climax until I came, shuddering and gasping, blasting jet after jet of hot fluid into my wife's mouth.

After I'd driven home, still trembling after the intensity of my orgasm, I tried to tackle Joanne again about what had happened.

It wasn't as if we didn't have a good sex life, but a daylight blowjob in the front seat of the car was hardly the norm.

She brushed the whole episode aside.

'It was the excitement, darling. The thought of living in that lovely house. We will buy it, won't we?'

'Well, maybe, but I think we should be careful before we jump straight into a deal. And we must let Julie see it first. She has to live there too.'

Joanne's face darkened for a moment then cleared.

'She'll love it too. I'll take her to see it tomorrow after you've gone to work.'

The following evening Julie, our sixteen-year-old daughter, declared the house to be 'cool' and the summerhouse, to my surprise, 'wicked'.

She and her mother chattered excitedly through dinner about the house. I had brought some files home from the office, and I stayed up working until late. I slipped quietly into bed, expecting Joanne to be asleep.

But, as I lay on my back with my eyes closed, I felt the mattress shift, and her fingers gently twisted the hair on my chest.

'See, sweetheart?' she whispered. 'I told you Julie

would love the house.'

Her fingers began a slow trip down to my stomach.

'Jo, I'm …'

Her lips closed over mine and her tongue slithered into my mouth. She took my cock in her hand while she rubbed her breasts across my chest.

The kiss grew more intense. She sucked my tongue into her hot mouth and moved her hand lower to cup my balls. She squeezed hard.

I grunted with pain and shock and she lifted her head.

'You're what, darling?'

She released my balls and a sharp fingernail touched my anus.

'Are you tired?'

My body jerked as she slid her finger inside me and began to massage, something she had never done before. My balls ached and my cock stood up like a steel rod. Her lips found my nipples, then her teeth bit down hard, and I gasped in pain.

Her finger slid out of me. She kissed me again, and I tasted salt on her lips.

'Come on. Quick!'

Her voice was harshly demanding.

I grabbed her, rolled her on to her back, and rammed my cock into her. Her cunt was soaking wet and hot and gripped me like a vice as I held my whole length still inside her.

I lifted myself up and looked down at her face in the faint light. Her eyes were tightly closed, her mouth was open and she wore an expression of pure lust that I had never seen before.

Sweat dripped off my chin and pooled in the hollow of her neck and I felt the muscles of her vagina working on my cock as I flexed it.

Her eyes flew open.

'Fuck me! Hard!'

I began to thrust. Her legs went high around my back and I felt a heel rub down my spine.

'Harder!'

I slammed into her as hard as I could and was dimly aware of the sound of the bedsprings twanging in rhythm with the headboard thumping against the wall.

Her body bucked frantically under mine as she thrust up to meet me. As I felt the familiar tingle of my orgasm beginning I looked down into Joanne's face. Her eyes were still closed and her lips were moving silently as she strained to reach her climax.

I fought to stay with her as she writhed under me and the orgasm built and built. The sweat was pouring from both of us and, just as I was feeling I could hold it no longer, she spoke. It was a strange gasping voice from deep inside her.

'Yes. Oh, yes. Thank you.'

Then she shouted: 'I'm coming! Oh fuck, fuck, fuck!'

Her eyes sprang open and she let out a long wailing cry. I felt myself going over the top and yelled as I exploded inside her. My cock pumped frantically and my muscles tensed as rush after rush of pleasure raced through me. She pulled me down on top of her and we lay together, blissfully sticky. The only sound was our heavy breathing. I slid out of her and rolled on to my back.

Her lips touched mine. 'I'm so looking forward to our new house, aren't you?' she whispered as I fell into a deep sleep.

Julie grinned impishly at me at breakfast. 'Sleep well last night, Dad?'

'Yes, thanks. Why?'

'Oh, I thought I heard you and mum *talking,* quite late.'

'Drink your juice. You'll be late for school.'

Buying the house became an obsession with Joanne. My natural caution told me to hold back, to consider other properties, but in truth it was ideal for our needs, with a big garden and Julie's new school close by. Joanne had a strong ally in our daughter and between the two of them I had little chance.

On top of that, the whole business seemed to have affected my wife's libido. Joanne had always had a healthy appetite for sex, but now she was urging me to do some of the things we'd done in the early years before our marriage – and some we'd only ever talked about.

A week after the blowjob incident, the agent rang to say the seller was prepared to drop the price of the house by five per cent for a quick sale.

With no real reason to refuse I agreed, and the contracts were exchanged that afternoon. We went out to dinner to celebrate. On the way home, Joanne had me drive to the spot where we used to make out as teenagers. In those days it had been a deserted spot by the river with long grass and bushes. Now it was a manicured riverbank, overlooked by a couple of high-rise apartment buildings. I stopped the car.

'Dare you,' she whispered.

'What?'

'I put a blanket in the trunk.'

'Oh, no. No way.'

She shifted closer to me, her lips pouting. 'This is the first place we did it.'

'It was a lot more private then. And we were a lot younger.' Her hand wriggled inside my pants. 'No,

Joanne. No, no, no!'

I'd forgotten how good fucking in the open air could be. I don't know if anyone was watching and, by the time I'd taken her panties off, I didn't care. We screwed like a couple of high school kids, still half dressed, squealing and groaning.

Joanne was quiet on the way home, deep in thought. 'Penny for them,' I said.

'Just savouring the memories, sweetheart.'

We moved into the house about two weeks later. The interior of the house and the garden needed a lot of attention and this, together with an increased workload at the office, meant my life was hectic. Joanne's libido subsided after we moved in, and I was rather thankful that our sex life had returned to normal. It was a while before I got around to paying any attention to the summerhouse. Julie had taken it upon herself to put a couple of chairs and an old settee inside, and she spent quite a lot of time there. Our daughter was growing up to be a very attractive young lady, and there was a persistent stream of boys vying for her affections.

The first time I decided to take a good look at the summerhouse I almost walked in on Julie and her latest admirer stretched out on the settee, their lips glued together and their hands exploring slowly. In bed that night I told Joanne and she laughed. 'What were you like at sixteen?'

'Yes, but what if …?'

'Rob, why don't you concentrate on where to put *your* hands … That's it … Just there. And there …'

Summer turned to fall, and red and gold leaves fell from the trees. The garden began to look bare and the summerhouse stood out, stark and ugly. I finally brought up the subject of knocking it down. We were sitting on the patio after lunch, on one of those warm golden days that late October sometimes brings. The reaction was quick and very definite. 'Oh, no, Dad.' Julie looked devastated. 'I love the summerhouse, and Rebecca ...'

She stopped abruptly at the look on her mother's face, and dropped her eyes to the tabletop. Joanne's face was white and her eyes were brilliant. 'Who's Rebecca, Julie?' Her voice was harsh.

'She's a school friend. She comes over sometimes. I don't think you've met her. She likes the summerhouse.' The words came out as if rehearsed. There was a long silence.

'Off you go, Julie. I want to talk to your mother.'

Julie stood, seemed about to say something, and then stalked away towards the summerhouse.

'What's going on, Jo? Who is Rebecca?'

Her face was pale, and she sat silent for a long time. When she spoke her voice was low. 'I'm not sure.' I opened my mouth to speak and she held up a hand to stop me. 'The name, Rob. It made me remember. I think...' Her voice tailed off.

I made my voice gentle. 'What do you think?'

'I think she's old and I think she's evil. And I think she was inside me!' The words rushed out, ending in a shout, and she burst into tears.

Slowly I coaxed it out of her. 'That first time in the summerhouse. When I came. It wasn't me, it was her. It was for her. And, when I sucked you in the car, she wanted to remember what it was like. She got inside me. All the crazy sex we've had, she wanted. To remember. Whatever she is, somehow she got inside me.'

The tears rolled down her cheeks and I stroked her hair. 'It's OK, baby. You've been fine since we moved here.'

'Yes, Rob, I have. But don't you see? She's here. In the summerhouse!'

I strode toward the summerhouse and was about to call out when I heard Julie's voice. 'My dad was going to knock your house down,' she said. 'But it's all right, I won't let him.'

She was sitting on the small veranda, and she jumped when she saw me. 'Who were you talking to?'

'No one, Dad. I was practising some lines for the school play.' I looked hard at her and her brilliant blue eyes met my gaze without flinching.

'OK,' I said, exasperated. 'Go on indoors.' As I watched her walking to the house there was a whisper of sound inside the summerhouse. I turned and opened the door. A small piece of bright red ribbon fluttered to the floor. Hesitantly, I stepped inside and picked it up. I ran it through my fingers, put it in my pocket and went into the house.

I told Joanne what had happened. '... and then I saw this ribbon,' I concluded, putting my hand in my pocket. The ribbon wasn't there.

We talked late into the night, trying to make sense of it all. Joanne was adamant that the summerhouse had to go. 'It's evil, Rob. Get it knocked down.'

'OK. I'll do it at the weekend.'

I told Julie what I intended to do the next morning, before I left for work. I expected tantrums but she simply stared wordlessly at me, then turned and walked into her room, closing the door softly behind her.

I arrived home late, just in time to see her getting into a car containing a gang of youngsters, which swept away with the sounds of loud music.

'She's gone to a party,' Joanne said. 'It's October 31st.' I stared blankly at her. 'Halloween, dumbo. Trick or treat. Remember?'

The events of the last few days had left Halloween the furthest thing from my mind.

'A party? Will she be OK? Who with? What's her curfew?'

Joanne burst out laughing. 'God, you sound just like my father used to.'

'But Jo, that boy the other day was practically undressing her. I think you'd better talk to her.'

'Rob, she's been on the pill for the last twelve months. She's very capable of looking after herself. And she'll be home by midnight.'

I gaped at her. 'On the pill? You mean she's not …'

'A virgin? She hasn't told me, but I very much doubt it. You can ask her if you like.'

I shook my head in disbelief.

The car pulled up outside at 11.45, doors opened and then closed again, softly. Joanne chuckled. 'Saying goodnight in the back seat, I fancy.'

It was ten minutes after midnight before Julie came in. Joanne smiled at her. 'Good party, sweetheart?'

'Fabulous, Mum.' Her face had a happy, dreamy look, as if she was far away. 'I'm tired though. I'm going to bed.'

She kissed us both quickly and disappeared to her bedroom. Joanne held out her hand to me. 'Come on, bedtime.' I lay sleepless, my thoughts racing. Joanne put her arm around me. 'Still worried about your daughter?'

'She's only sixteen, Jo.'

'So how old were you the first time?'

Her hand crept down my stomach and my cock began to harden. 'I've told you. Sixteen. But that's different.'

'Why? I was only seventeen the first time you took my panties off.' She took my cock in her hand and stroked it. 'Come on, sweetheart. I want this guy inside me.' She took my hand and guided it down between her legs. She was hot and wet and she moaned as my fingers tickled her clit. 'See how much I want you?'

We made love slowly, losing control only at the end, and came together in a sudden, blissful rush.

I woke from a nightmare of smoke and flames and lay still, watching the red light flickering on the walls of the room until I suddenly realised it was no longer a dream. I leapt to the window and ripped the curtains aside. The summerhouse was a mass of flames. I shook Joanne violently, hauled on a pair of jeans and ran to the door.

'Find Julie!'

I tore downstairs, out of the kitchen door. The heat hit me before I had gone more than a few yards. Flames were exploding from the hut and sparks showered into the air. I turned, ran back into the house and grabbed the phone as Joanne screamed from the landing, 'Rob! She's not here!'

I rushed back outside to see the whole structure cave in with a huge bang. Flames shot heavenward and the garden became a glare of orange light. As my eyes refocused, I saw a shimmering light and watched a small figure emerge from the inferno and skip away across the garden – a little girl with long black hair tied with a bright red ribbon.

There was an enquiry of course, but it revealed little. All that was left of Julie were teeth and some bone fragments in the ashes – enough for a DNA test.

I never told Joanne what I saw that night. We separated a year later and divorced a year after that.

The whisky helps.

The Pirates
by Carmel Lockyer

I should have known the day Lucy rang me that I was about to get tricked into something. A call from my twin sister meant nothing but trouble.

'Laurie,' she trilled into the phone. 'We're going to have such fun. The local operatic society is putting on *The Pirates of Penzance* – on an actual boat! Isn't that magnificent?'

Lucy has always wanted to be an actress. Even though she trained as a drama teacher she's never given up the idea of making it to the big screen. I've always wanted to be a caterer – and guess what? One of us actually achieved their ambition, although to hear Lucy talk about it, you'd think she was the success and me the failure. 'My sister the sandwich maker,' she calls me.

'No,' I said.

I was still saying it a week later as we headed for auditions in the village hall. Lucy had found the perfect inducement for me. If we were cast as two of the daughters in the opera, she would make sure I got the catering contract for the opening night.

The plot to *The Pirates of Penzance* is so silly I couldn't understand it. The pirates are all so soft-hearted they are crap at their task; a servant apprentices the orphan baby she's taking care of to them – thinking they are pilots. He's called Frederick, grows up and declares that when his apprenticeship is over he will hunt down all the pirates because he's a proper decent gentleman. He falls in love with a general's daughter, the pirates come and kidnap all the other general's daughters … oh you get the picture – sheer rubbish. The tunes are good though.

Of course Lucy and I were shoo-ins for daughters: even if we hadn't been able to sing we'd have got the parts, because 21-year-old identical twin girls nearly always do get what they want. So we were sent off with our sheet music and our librettos (that's opera for lines) and told to come back three days later to meet the principals.

On the way home, Lucy decided to detour to the boat where the performances would take place. It was a wooden fishing boat, lovingly restored by some local eccentric, and although most of the opera would be performed on a stage built in front of it, some of Frederick's solos and the pirate choruses would be sung on the boat itself. I hoped they wouldn't expect my waiting staff to prepare the nibbles and champagne on board too – the galley wasn't big enough to iron a pair of pants in.

That night I had the most peculiar dream. I was tied to the mast of the boat, and a curly-haired pirate was running his rapier up and down my body. That's not a euphemism, it was an icy cold metal blade and everywhere it touched me it left a line of goosebumps followed by a warm shuddery pleasure. He'd just drawn the tip of the rapier to a point between my legs and was curling his moustache with his free hand while he laughed, when I woke up.

The really odd thing is I don't like men, pirates or otherwise. The one reason Lucy and I get on so well is she's mad for anything in trousers and I prefer women – otherwise we'd be at each other's throats, of course, because just about every man you meet has this fantasy about twins taking him to bed, but Lucy's boyfriends don't bother to hit on me more than once.

When we met the principal singers I understood why Lucy was so keen on opera all of a sudden. Frederick was as swarthy and curly haired as the man in my dream, and every time he looked over at us, my sister became hot and bothered. There was a nice old man with a voice like good whisky who was playing the General, our 'father', and half a dozen other men who'd been cast as pirates. Ruth, the old nurse who gives Frederick to the pirate crew, was an elderly lady who'd been funding the operatic society since forever. It was all as I'd expected, until the pirate chief came out. He was a she! It was my turn to blush and shuffle my feet: I'd never seen such a gorgeous, terrifying woman – she was as piratical as Blackbeard but much better looking. I sneaked to the back of the stage and hid behind some scenery so I could observe her better. She had platinum hair, cropped to brutal shortness, dark eyes that were challenging and somehow amused by everything she saw and a lush mouth, coated in crimson lipstick. I thought about how it would feel to have her lips pressed to my body, and shuddered. Unfortunately my shiver of desire transmitted itself to the fake pillar I was standing behind and it toppled over.

Every head in the place turned to me. The only one I noticed was hers. She raked me up and down with a cruel sardonic glance and turned away. She had a tight, well-muscled rear, I noticed, although by now I was cherry red and almost in tears of embarrassment: the look she'd given me was contemptuous and it stung.

I worked hard on my lines, knowing that the pirate chief, Ellen, would be merciless to any singer who wasn't up to her standards. I'd heard her sing and she had a fine voice. I imagined her murmuring 'Laurie, Laurie' then told myself to concentrate. She wasn't interested in me and if I didn't want a tongue-lashing at the next rehearsal I'd better be word and note perfect.

That night I dreamed of the pirate boat again, but this time Lucy was tied to the mast being teased by the cutlass of my platinum-haired pirate woman. I was trying to get to them, explaining that she'd got the wrong daughter, but my arms were pinned behind my back by Frederick, who was murmuring 'Lucy, Lucy' in my ear. Very Freudian, I thought when I woke up. I spent the day packing picnic hampers for a company that rents out punts on the river – they're one of my best clients and I try to take good care of them – but I kept getting distracted, staring out the window to the mast of the fishing boat that I could just see in the distance, and wondering if there was any way the pirate chief might notice me. She looked butch enough to be lesbian, or at least bi, and I was so smitten that I began to imagine scenarios where I converted her to the womanly arts and she expressed her gratefulness with strong brutal fingers and punishing kisses. When I got to the point of adding in a strap-on shaped like a ship's figurehead I looked down and realised I'd just made twenty-four avocado and jam sandwiches. Not good. I tried one. They actually didn't taste too bad, but there was no way I could put them in hampers, so in the bin they went.

We had a rehearsal the following evening and before we drove down to the hall we were using to practise, I went through Lucy's wardrobe, trying to find something that was both sexy and suitable – catering doesn't require much of a wardrobe. The problem was that a General's daughter was going to end up wearing not much more than a floral sack in the performances, so any impressing I was going to do would have to happen in rehearsals. Lucy looked wonderful in a pink cashmere sweater and leather trousers, and I opted for a crisp white shirt with no bra underneath and a pair of soft velvet pants in burgundy. The pirate chief never even looked my way, although Frederick could hardly keep his eyes, or hands, off Lucy.

That night I dreamed of Lucy and Frederick: the pirate chief made them walk the plank into a vat of jam and once in, they had one of those slo-mo mud fights so beloved of soft porn films, rolling around in the pink stickiness until they looked like a couple of figures made of Turkish Delight. Then all the pirates and the General's other daughters licked them clean, pirates on Lucy and daughters on Frederick. I stood at the back, holding a tray of lemonade and buns. Even my dreams were letting me down.

I went through the box under my bed before heading to work. I hadn't bothered with it for a while, not being involved with anyone, and I'd forgotten a lot of what was in there: a couple of pink silk ropes for tying to bedposts; a glass dildo in a padded box; Ben Wa balls; emotion lotion in hot and icy; a pair of transparent tunics that Shauna and I had worn to a fancy dress party when we were a couple ... I wondered where Shauna was now, and whether she was having more fun than me. A pair of sky-high black stilettos with laces that came up above my knees; a pheromone spray, guaranteed to attract women.

I left the spray on the bathroom shelf – I was pretty sure it didn't work but nothing else seemed to be working either. Ellen wasn't a pirate chief; she was a pirate ice queen.

At our next rehearsal she bawled me out. It wasn't my fault, but she did it anyway. Lucy and Frederick had sneaked off somewhere and when Ellen was ready to sing her duet with him, he was nowhere to be found. I just happened to pass across the hall and she bellowed, 'You – Lolo or whatever your name is, if you can't take rehearsals more seriously then step down and let a serious singer take your place.'

I hid in the yard until the rest had gone. I heard Lucy come looking for me but I didn't let her know where I was. I was so angry with her, and so humiliated, I couldn't have spoken anyway. There are people who get off on being humiliated, apparently – I'm not one of them; every time I thought about Ellen I nearly burst into tears, and the idea that everybody in the hall had heard her tongue-lash me was unendurable. Lucy could do what she liked but they were going to have to find another General's daughter to replace me, they could stuff their opera wherever it fitted and I hoped it hurt.

I drove home in a fury of emotions to find Ellen standing on my doorstep. I straightened my back as I approached her. 'Don't worry,' I said. 'I can take a hint. I won't be appearing in *Pirates of Penzance*.' I hoped it sounded ironic.

She leaned towards me. I could smell her perfume, spicy and warm like cranberries. 'Honey, I mixed you up with your sister. Forgive me?'

I stared into her dark eyes. She fully expected to be forgiven: she wasn't at all contrite. In fact she looked almost amused.

'If you want forgiveness, it's yours. But I don't need that kind of hassle and I don't like being told off in public. Your manners are shitty.'

She blinked as I pushed past her and fitted my key in the door. 'Ouch! I guess I deserve that. You're right, I have a habit of telling people what to do – should've left it to the director but, to be honest, he's a little bit smitten with your twin and he'd never have said anything.'

I thought about that for a second. Lucy did get away with a lot, and she had let everybody down. I turned to Ellen, to say I accepted her apology, but before I could speak she grabbed my chin and kissed me, full and open.

'See, I do have good manners too,' she said over her shoulder, as she strode back down the path. I was too weak-kneed to comment.

I expected to dream that night, but I didn't. Instead I spent the whole of the next day, when I was making raised-crust summer pies, remembering the feel of Ellen's mouth on mine.

Lucy turned up after school, to tell me all about the hot night she'd spent with Frederick. Apparently he was kinkier than a barbed wire fence and he'd even tied her to the bed and caressed her with his prop sword. I didn't tell her I knew all about it, having dreamt it more than a week ago. I just listened in silence until she ran out of words.

'Lucy, if you mess up one more time, then I'm never doing anything with you again. Understand? I'm taking this opera seriously and I want you to as well.'

She pouted at me, 'Just 'cos your pirate queen won't play your game, don't take it out on me.'

I smiled, leaving her in no doubt she was wrong, but refused to go into details. 'Pirate's code of honour' was all I said when she pressed me, but really, a kiss was such a little thing that I knew she wouldn't be impressed.

That night Ellen was on my doorstep at seven. 'Ask me in?' she suggested. I held the door open.

She sat on my old couch and pulled me down beside her. 'Honey, I'm a professional singer. I can't afford to muddy the waters here. Anything between you and me has to wait until this show is over – understand?'

I understood and I kept my thoughts and hands to myself.

The opera was a huge success. On opening night Frederick took all the skin off his hands slipping down a rope in the rigging and had to appear in bandages in every subsequent performance. The General kept forgetting what opera we were doing and launching into *HMS Pinafore* instead, and three of the pirates regularly got seasick and had to perform their parts on shore instead of on the boat, but the audiences lapped it up, just as they did the champagne and strawberries I served in the intermission.

The last night was a packed house, well, a packed green. We ended the show with all of us trooping on to the boat and vanishing below decks while fireworks went off. It was like playing Sardines in a wooden can: we were all crammed together and giggling like crazy – the General definitely had his hand under nurse Ruth's skirt in the dark, and Lucy and Frederick were so tangled together you couldn't tell where the pirate ended and the General's daughter began. Lucy was shameless; out of the corner of my eye I could see her lifting the back of her skirt as she stood in front of Frederick and he unbuttoned his pirate trews and slipped inside her. Every time a firework went off he thrust into her and she gasped – and when the climax of the performance arrived, my wicked sister wriggled on his fleshy sword

107

until she climaxed too.

We all waited until the last car had driven out of the lot, and then piled back on deck to celebrate. Lucy had told me there would be little skits and performances by many of the cast and we'd prepared our own, just to be sociable. Under our floral dresses we were wearing the diaphanous tunics from the fancy dress do.

The General sang a dirty ditty about sailors frigging in the rigging, three of the pirates performed 'I Should Be So Lucky' in falsetto Kylie voices, completed with a suggestive dance that was hilarious alongside their eye patches and hairy chests, and nurse Ruth told jokes that had us creased up. Then Lucy and I took to the stage. We sang 'Sisters' of course, but the singing was only incidental to the almost transparent mini-dresses and the way we clung together, passing our hands over each other's hips and breasts. Sometimes there are advantages to being a twin.

Lucy kept her eyes on Frederick and I watched Ellen who was observing sardonically. At the end of our performance we got a standing ovation, only interrupted when Ellen strode onto the stage. She was still wearing her pirate costume.

'These two need cooling down!' she yelled. 'Let's make them walk the plank!' My mouth opened in shock, could the woman read my mind? Next thing I knew, the whole cast was hustling us to the ship's side, and Lucy and I were in the water. It wasn't deep but it was cold and we were spluttering a little as they pulled us back out again, and stood us dripping on the deck.

'Now!' Ellen said. 'Pirates are notoriously wicked, aren't they?'

The crew yelled in appreciation.

'So let's get wicked! I'm going to auction these two

lovelies, one at a time, to the highest bidder. So let's start with ...' her eyes met mine and she winked. 'Lucy!'

Frederick won, of course, although it would have been cheaper for him to take my sister to the most expensive restaurant in town, in a hired limo, and shower her in champagne. Then it was my turn. I stood, shivering slightly, in my now totally transparent tunic.

'Was that fun?' Ellen yelled.

The audience yelled back that it was.

'Good! Then we'll do something different this time – Laurie will be going home with the person who climbs to the top of the mast fastest. General?'

The old man looked up.

'Act as timekeeper please.'

Only three men decided they could face the climb. I looked up at the mast; it was pretty high and I hoped none of them would make it, suddenly this wasn't fun at all. I tried to say something to Ellen but she picked up her curving pirate sword and pointed it between my breasts. 'Silence, captive,' she said.

The first man got no more than eight feet from the deck. The second managed about twelve. The third actually made it to the top. I resigned myself to an evening of pushing his hands away and arguing with him about exactly what he'd won.

Then Ellen pulled off her pirate jacket and rolled up her sleeves. She shinned up the mast in no time at all. To cheers and jeers she descended to the deck and grabbed my arm. 'Pirate treasure,' she cackled in a harsh voice, and the audience whistled their appreciation.

She had a big towel and a flask of hot chocolate in the car. 'You knew you were going to win,' I said accusingly.

'Of course,' she said.

Funnily enough, I didn't feel at all flattered. When we got back to the little flat she had been renting for the duration of the opera, I stood like a wet fish in the hall, wishing I could go home alone.

Ellen knelt in front of me, pulling me towards her. I could feel the heat of her breath through my panties. Her hands went to my buttocks, nails dragging gently across them and down my thighs. I started to shudder. Slowly she lifted the tunic and pressed her mouth to my navel, leaving a red blossom around it. 'Pirate's kiss,' she murmured. I was starting to feel better about the evening. I set my hands on her short hair and tipped her head up, bending down so I could kiss her full on the lips. She sighed and then stood up, leading me to her bedroom.

In my bag I had the pheromone spray but I didn't think I was going to need it. As she tugged at my underwear with frantic hands I reached down and stopped her. 'Did you bring your cutlass?' I asked.

She raised a sardonic eyebrow. 'Why?'

'Oh, well, I had a dream you see, and I thought it might be fun to act it out.'

She smiled elegantly. 'I don't think captives get to tell pirates what to do.'

I nodded in agreement. 'But don't captives get tied to things and threatened with horrible punishments?'

She laughed.

So that's why, after a little while, I found myself bound to Ellen's bed, with a buxom pirate straddling me, cutlass in one hand. I pushed my hips up to allow her fingers easier entry and as she thrust her hand into me she sang one of the General's daughters' lines: 'Will no one in his cause a weapon wield?' I could have replied but I was too busy enjoying the sensation of her strong fingers opening me.

Maybe I'm not cut out to be an opera star, but when I orgasmed I'm sure I hit high C.

Saint Valentine
by Donna George Storey

Voluptuous.

The word's a mouthful, but it feels so nice on the tongue. Like me.

I could lose ten pounds, but when I put on my skinny jeans and a plunging V-neck shirt, even men with rail-thin cover girls on their arms can't tear their eyes away. Once they get me naked, their lips are drawn to me like magnets, devouring my full breasts, licking my white, rounded belly like ice cream, gliding to rest in the tender cleft of my secret flesh. *Creamy*, they whisper, *luscious*. Beneath the husky words, I hear their true longing: a primal, almost carnivorous lust for female flesh.

Yet, although my bed is always warm with satisfied men, I haven't quite found that one special guy. Still I've always liked being a delicious dish. Until now.

The problem is that I've fallen in love with a vegan.

To be honest, it's more 'in lust'. I met Justin two months ago when he joined our theatre troupe as the lighting director. I flirt with him outrageously, but that is my specialty. On stage I play the vamps, the lusty barmaids, the whorehouse madams in crimson bustiers. All the roles a full-figured temptress plays to perfection. Justin flirts back, but I sense a reserve, as if he means to stay above life's coarser urges. After rehearsal, when we all go off to the pub to polish off pitchers of microbrew and potato skins with bacon and sour cream, Justin takes a seat at the end of the table and sips a single glass of red wine.

Though I chug and gobble with the rest of them, I secretly admire my vegan saint. I find his willingness to deny himself carnal gratification for a higher principle unbearably sexy. But, because I really am a bad girl at heart, I also want to defile his purity, pull him down onto my hot, rumpled sheets for a fleshly feast that lasts for nights on end.

Which is probably why I couldn't get up the nerve to ask him out – good, old-fashioned Catholic-girl guilt.

Fortunately, Justin is a Buddhist.

'Would you like to come to my place for dinner Thursday night?' He pops the question as I'm lounging backstage, waiting for my next scene.

'That's Valentine's Day,' I say, without thinking.

'Yes. Do you have other plans?'

Nothing I couldn't cancel to get a mouthful of you. That's what I think, what I say is, 'I was just planning to hang out at home hoping a prince would ride by with some chocolate and roses.'

'You're not going to let candy corporations and florists brainwash you with their profit-making fantasies, are you?' He smiles, but I sense he's not really kidding.

'It just so happens I like chocolate and flowers. I even buy them for myself now and then,' I say, looking him straight in the eye. 'Of course, you probably think I'm a dupe of consumer capitalism with my silly dreams.'

He holds my gaze steadily for what seems like for ever. His eyes flicker with a tiny golden flame, warming me, melting me. I realise I haven't breathed in quite some time.

'Well,' he says finally, 'I hope a wholesome, organic meal with a nice wine will be an acceptable alternative to that propaganda.'

I swallow and nod, strangely at a loss for words. But although I'm acting like a love-sick female, in one tiny corner of my mind, I'm still as clear and calculating as ever. Why not accept his invitation? There's a risk Justin might spend the night lecturing me on organic farming techniques and corporate manipulation of consumers, but there's an upside, too. It's also my golden chance to slither my way inside his monk's cell – and hopefully his bed. With temptations of the flesh so near, even he might find it impossible to resist my generous charms.

Instead temptation comes to visit me in my bed. That night I dream I'm lying on my back on some kind of stone slab, my thighs spread wide like a virgin sacrifice. Justin stands before me, wearing priestly black and a serene smile. Then his gaze falls to my pussy, swollen and exposed, and suddenly the smile stretches into satyr's leer. I try to sit up or at least pull my gauzy shift down to cover myself, but I discover I'm bound to the slab, totally at his mercy.

My pussy tingles and throbs and a warm wetness trickles under my thighs. I know I'm shamefully aroused down there, and Justin knows it, too. He's staring at me with glowing eyes and licking his lips with a moist red tongue. Just then liquid dribbles from the corner of his mouth, not drool but something opalescent and viscous like jism. He bends to taste my offering, grinning and slobbering, and in spite of myself my hips arch up to meet him. I know his terrible transformation from saint to sinner is my fault. Though my body is twitching and trembling in anticipation of that nimble tongue on my secret lips, a scream rises in my chest – *Stop! You don't eat meat!* – but no sound comes.

I wake up drenched in sweat, troubled, but undeniably horny. Dipping my hand between my legs to masturbate, I pretend my finger is Justin's greedy tongue, lapping and licking with devotion. I imagine him kneeling down there between my legs, his head bobbing slightly as he works me over. I hear the click of my wet flesh as he feasts, savour the vision of him pausing to smile up at me to whisper – *delicious*--his lips and chin shimmering with my juices in the moonlight. When I climax, I make plenty of noise, partly because it's hot jilling off to the thought of Justin's mouth on my pussy, partly to reassure myself dreams don't always come true.

Then again, sometimes they do.

Come Valentine's Day I discover my monk's cell is not at all how I imagined it would be. The apartment is sparsely furnished, but it has a Japanese-inspired elegance that catches me off-guard. Dinner is another surprise. I expected seitan and sprouts, but he serves me a lavish salad of organic greens, porcini risotto, and a subtly earthy Sicilian wine. Dessert is almost decadent: four different bars of fair-trade dark chocolate that Justin suggests we taste in a flight like wine.

Who am I to deny him anything?

We sit side by side on his futon sofa. I notice a spray of plum blossom arranged gracefully in a vase-like basket on the end table.

'I hope you didn't patronize an evil capitalist flower shop for this?'

'Oh, no, I clipped a branch from the tree in the back yard. The most beautiful things can't be bought.' He smiles into my eyes.

115

'No,' I admit in a faint voice. It's almost shameless how quickly he's brought me under his spell with his pure-minded sensuality.

He breaks off a piece of the first chocolate bar and holds it to my lips.

Bewitched by the wine, his smile, the cinnamon smell of his skin, I part my lips and accept it like a communion wafer.

He smiles, serenely, then bends to bless me with a kiss. The wafer turns to a cocoa cordial between our dancing tongues – slick, intoxicating, impious.

When the chocolate is gone, Justin reaches over and turns off the Japanese lamp.

'How will we know what we're tasting in the dark?'

'You'll be the light,' Justin whispers. 'Don't you know you illuminate the whole theatre every time you walk on stage?'

I laugh. He's been softening me with compliments all evening. Here on his turf, he has a charm that is positively dangerous to a woman's virtue. Not that I have any left. I'm ready to rip off my clothes for him then and there, but Justin has beaten me to it, lifting my V-neck shirt over my head, unsnapping my black lace bra.

Now I learn yet another secret. A monk really is just like other men. He catches his breath as my breasts fall free. His eyes sparkle when he discovers how sensitive my nipples are to the ministrations of his fingers and tongue.

I'm the one who is different. Though I squirm and sigh and beg him to touch my pussy like I always do, my body feels oddly weightless in his arms. It must be the dinner, an elixir of organic vegetables coursing through my veins like liquid sunshine. I'm so caught up in the pure, buoyant sensation, I hardly notice Justin has me out of my jeans and is kneeling on the floor, parting my thighs.

He leans forward, his lips moist, his face flushed. His eyes flash with naked desire for my raw pink flesh.

My dream really is about to come true.

I realise with a pang that I've done this to him, brought him to his knees. My chest tightens. I don't want him to be like the others.

But this isn't a dream and I am able speak.

'But Justin,' I falter, 'you don't eat meat.'

A smile floats to his lips as he traces my slippery-slick groove with his fingertip. 'I never understood why they call women such things. Meat or fish-and-finger pie. You're not meat, Melissa. You're a flower, with moist lovely petals.' He leans in and teases my clit with the tip of his tongue. Pausing, he looks up at me, his lips shining faintly. 'You're a ripe fruit, still warm from the sun.'

Voluptuous, delectable, a fine piece of ass. My flesh has been described in many ways, but never so sweetly. And so I don't protest when he bends to feast in earnest. I lounge back on the sofa and spread my legs wider so his tongue can savour the plump little berry of my clit. Instinctively my hips tilt up to him, like a flower to the sun.

One hand slides over my belly to my breast. He tweaks the nipple, which stiffens, a strawberry candy floating in the creamy expanse of my breast. His other hand creeps up between my thighs, then farther back to that forbidden and exquisitely sensitive hole behind. There he strokes me as he might the furry skin of a peach.

I shudder and squirm with pleasure. He flicks my clit

117

faster and the clicking sound of tongue on flesh fills the room. I'm so wet, so very wet, I must be flooding his upholstery, but I'm too deeply aroused to feel any shame. My body is opening, blossoming. His tongue lashes me now, electric jolts shoot from his fingers at my nipple straight down to my anus, where he teases and tickles mercilessly. My belly pulses, a ball of heat swelling deep inside me. The heat grows, a golden warmth spreading out through my body to my fingertips and toes. I'm so light, so radiant, I finally lift right off the sofa, rocketing skyward in a burst of pure enlightenment.

There's a lot to be said for the pleasures of the vegan life after all.

Afterwards I gaze at Justin's face. He smiles, his chin glistening with my juices. I see now he's no self-denying monk. He's a gourmet, a romantic, and the best pussy-licker I've ever met. But he's still a saint to me.

Saint Valentine.

Moistened by Mercer
by Jeremy Edwards

I've always felt a deep-seated craving to know which of the women around me think I'd be worth taking to bed. Mind you, they don't have to actually *take* me to bed. They don't even have to kiss me on the cheek or hold my hand or e-mail me animated valentines. But I do have a compulsion to find out whether or not they consider me sexually attractive. Do their pussies ever get a little wet when I smile at them? Do they ever think about me when they touch themselves? I desperately want to know these things, and I have no right to know these things. So let's just say such knowledge is a 'privilege'. A privilege, ladies and gentlemen, that I vigorously pursue.

I've been told that I'm handsome, in an offbeat way. I've been told that I'm charming, and it's whispered here and there that I'm sort of sexy. But I'm not the type who has the whole room swooning at his feet. My charisma pollinates the ecosystem, and flowers of feminine excitement blossom here and there – not everywhere.

My consuming curiosity regarding my fuckability pertains primarily to women I work with, women in my circle of friends and other women with whom I have some greater or lesser degree of regular interaction. The women who work at the café I frequent. The women I always see on the bus. I look at someone and secretly wonder if she senses in me that special, undefined zest that can make a girl light up downstairs. Does my face ever flicker across her mind while her fingers flit around her clit? This is not the kind of question one comes right out and asks; and yet questions of that type are, perennially, the most compelling questions in my heart.

I do also wonder about women whom I encounter on a more ephemeral basis. A woman behind the cash register at a shop I'll never return to. A woman I pass once on the street. Did something tingle when we made eye contact? In these cases, I'll never know. In these cases, I'm forced to imagine. Usually, when I get home, I choose to imagine that the angelic face I passed on the street is now contorted into a sexual grimace as she sits in her own home, fingers moist, imagining that I throb reciprocally for her. I get myself off by fantasising about the stranger fantasising about me while she gets *herself* off. Fair enough, right?

When I worked at the advertising agency, the assortment of smart, interesting women there represented a collection of respected colleagues and, in many instances, cherished pals. But they also, I must confess, represented a parade of female hormones. I was obsessed with what was between their legs, specifically as it did – or didn't – relate to the influence felt by my presence.

Once in a while, I got involved. But I was usually content to simply enjoy their friendly, casual company in the office, or at agency parties. Nonetheless, sooner or later, I generally managed to gauge – from facial expressions, body language, blushes or second-hand gossip – which of them thought I was hot. Once I was confident that someone did, in fact, get a tingle from me, then I felt especially justified in taking the information home to masturbate upon.

I was popular with my colleagues, but I assumed that many of them would have been a little put off if they'd known how often their buddy Mercer wondered whether their pussies were wet on his account.

But not Brenda. I didn't think Brenda would be put off. There was just something about her.

Brenda, I speculated, had moist panties whenever we interacted. This was not as self-congratulatory a judgment as it might sound – because Brenda, I speculated, had moist panties virtually all the time. As I said, there was just something about her. And yet I took a special pride in thinking that the specific moistness she was enjoying when we were in the same room was triggered by my magnetism. There was a certain sparkle to her expression, particularly when I made her laugh, which suggested that she might fancy eating my personality up like an erotic ice cream cone – and that I would love every minute of it.

Day after day, I went hard on company time by surmising that Brenda's knickers were moistening freshly for *me*. And I did as much as I could to be lively and engaging around her, without going so far as to make a lampshade-wearing nuisance of myself. I fantasised about broaching an intimacy with her – about having her breath in my face, and my hands in her panties. About inhaling the delirious fragrance of her flesh, where the backs of her thighs emerged from the miniskirts she frequently wore.

One day we were both making photocopies, at twin machines housed in a small room set aside for this purpose. We were chatting and joking, the way co-workers who get along well often do. And, as usual, I was convinced I was making Brenda wet. She was a bit flushed, and her hips seemed to rock ever so subtly as she shuffled her pages and pushed her buttons.

After a few minutes, I detected the enticing scent of Brenda's pussy cutting through the distasteful photocopying odours. Pre-cum in my shorts conclusively declared her a winner of my grandest lust, and I had to resist the temptation to rub myself against my copier in a frenzy of male excitation. Oh, how I wanted to fuck her, right then and there. The top of either photocopier would do – I wasn't choosy.

But, to be honest, I wasn't quite that spontaneous, either. So, rather than grabbing Brenda's mesmerising bottom and suggesting, through actions rather than words, that it would be a splendid idea to get my hard cock inside her flowing pussy before one more page of anything got duplicated ... I just kept up the chatter.

'I'm going to be sad when this party's over,' I remarked. 'How many pages do you have left?'

'I think around seventy-five,' she said. 'You?'

'Also looks like around seventy-five. Hey, maybe we should have a race.'

Brenda laughed. 'You *do* have a knack for making office life fun, don't you?'

My dick thrilled as she glanced up from her machine to twinkle at me. Little did she know how fun I *really* wanted to make it, at that particular moment. Or maybe she did know.

'Sure, Merce, let's race.' She giggled again. 'What does the victor get?'

'Well – ha ha – are sexual favours off limits?' This was more my style than an unanticipated hoisting of a friend onto the top of a photocopier: easing into it, within the context of some light-hearted kidding around.

'You're a dirty old man, Mercer.'

'Check,' I said. 'Isn't everyone?'

'No,' she reasoned crisply. 'I, for example, am not a man.'

Looking over her scrumptious anatomy, I acknowledged to myself that she had an excellent point. 'And not dirty?' I asked – teasing, because I was pretty damn sure she was even dirtier than I was.

'I didn't say that.'

After this, we found ourselves in a brief, amicable stare-down. Brenda, smirking, broke eye contact first.

As for the third term – 'old' – well, she and I were both in our thirties, and thus perhaps too young to have truly earned an 'old' to complement our 'dirty'. But this was not the time to worry about that. This was the time to keep making photocopies, as efficiently as one could with a piece of iron in one's trousers.

Besides, I assured myself, 'dirty old' was a state of mind. You're as 'dirty old' as you feel.

Our machines chugged away, and I noticed how their rhythms were in sync, like the grinds and grunts of a pair of well-matched lovers. This observation, needless to say, wasn't doing anything to diminish my hard-on. But I didn't want it to diminish. I wanted to feel it burning a hole in my shorts, a smouldering answer to the deliciously raunchy aroma Brenda had cooking under her skirt.

She finished first. 'Ha! I win the pissing contest!' she proclaimed while clearing the machine of her materials. Her choice of words made my mind reel with a kinky vision.

'Well done,' I said graciously through my lewd reverie. 'We never exactly determined the prize, did we?'

'No,' she said. 'Not exactly.' She blushed.

And then she did it. She hopped on top of her copier.

I was delighted to see that the door to this room had a lock. As I snapped it into place, I wondered if we were not the first couple to take advantage of this feature.

When I turned back from the door, she already had her panties off. She had tossed them over onto the lid of my machine; the effect was as if someone was planning on making fifteen copies of Brenda's moist underwear.

Her shoes were on the floor, her skirt was bunched up and the inviting succulence of her auburn-furred pussy was displayed for me within saucy thighs.

Her ankles dangled playfully, and I stepped forward and took hold of them. 'You're the victor,' I emphasised, as I let the fingers of my left hand tickle her where I clasped her. 'Do you want to be eaten or fucked?'

'Here's the thing, Mercer,' she said with a forced calmness, 'I've been thinking it over. And, you know, I beat your time by quite a bit. You must still have a dozen pages to do. In view of that, I think I'm entitled to be both eaten *and* fucked. Does that seem fair to you?'

I had to agree that this seemed perfectly fair.

She shrieked when my face dove into her skirt. Fortunately, the fan that constantly ran in this room – to help dissipate the copier fumes – provided a nice blanket of white noise beneath which we could, within reason, indulge our animalistic inclinations to be sexual out loud.

'I'm so wet for you,' she murmured as I began to tongue her. 'You're a real panty-soaker, Mercer.'

Those were the words I liked to hear.

The copier creaked on its haunches as her ass bounced sensuously atop it. She was, indeed, very wet for me; her pussy was so generous in its liquid tribute that I could barely keep up. Some of the juice that evaded my overworked tongue clung mischievously to my chin, while some pooled in a sassy, sticky puddle on the cool plastic lid of the machine.

Brenda was ticklish in there, all giggly folds tucked between chuckling thighs. And when I sucked on her jolly clit, the orgasm was half scream and half guffaw. It was beautiful.

She thought I was fuckable, and now it was time to prove her right. I removed my shoes and trousers and placed them neatly out of the way. My cock was so engorged that it took some doing to manoeuvre it through the slit in my boxers. Once it protruded, I felt ready for the shag of my life.

I took hold of the squishy femininity of Brenda's ass cheeks to scoot her forward. She sat up to greet me and, reaching for my rod, took charge of the penetration. As I plunged into her, she rubbed her naked heels up and down the backs of my legs, tickling herself on my coarse hairs and spurring me to even deeper thrusts. She – speaking of fuckableness – was a writhing pot of fuckability, and I had never, ever felt so good all over. Her body in my hands, around my legs and all over my cock displaced all consciousness of anything else I'd ever done. As I came for her, I poked the tip of a forefinger into her sexy asshole and whimpered my bliss into a hot little ear.

We'd made a wet, sticky, wonderful mess of the copier room. Brenda had been thoroughly moistened by Mercer, and Mercer had been expertly drained and stained by Brenda.

'What a mess,' she laughed, echoing my thoughts.

'Yes,' I said, breathing hard. 'And I have a few rooms at home that I'd like to see get messed up along these same lines. So what are you doing this weekend?'

'Making a mess,' Brenda said matter-of-factly, as she squeezed my flaccid cock with eager fingers.

Kiss Me in the Car
by Mimi Elise

Jason flicked his mobile shut and sighed impatiently. Outside the moon was bright, and a faint frost nipped the air. They'd broken down on a country lane, on their way back from a boring function, where they'd had too little to eat and, in Shelley's case, too much to drink while trying to look interested in the sales figures for Jason's company. But even the party was better than being stuck out in the middle of nowhere.

'The recovery truck should be here in about an hour,' he said. 'Might be sooner, but they can't promise. Bloody car. Why tonight of all nights? You'd think with how much it cost, it wouldn't let us down like this. And I've got to be up in the morning to drive to London.'

'What are we going to do to pass the time?' asked Shelley, hopefully. He was in such a bad mood he didn't hear the suggestion in her voice. She bit her lip, disappointed when he just shrugged.

'I suppose we'll have to just wait. We daren't put the radio on, in case the battery goes flat.'

What had happened to him? A few years ago he'd have been full of ideas, most of them involving taking off their clothes. 'Hmm,' she giggled, still woozy from the wine served with dinner. 'Remember your old Capri?

It's funny, but Mum was always alert to whether or not I had love bites, yet never noticed the bruises on my knees and elbows from trying to shag in that car.' She saw the gleam in his eyes, and knew at that moment that she had him. She felt his fingers press into her thigh and a dirty thrill she hadn't known since their children were born. 'How long is it since we made love in the back of the car?' she asked.

'Too long. But we're sensible grown-ups now,' he whispered against her ear. 'Far too mature for making out in the back seat. That's what teenagers do.' If that was the case, Shelley wished she were a teenager again. Things were less complicated then. She sensed that he still hesitated. What on earth had happened to him? And what could she do to take him back to those days when they didn't give a damn?

'Yet this one has nice leather seats. It's a pity to waste them,' she said. 'Leather on bare skin … there's nothing like it. Or so I'm told.' She pressed her bare shoulders against the seat, to test out her own theory. 'Very nice,' she said. 'Now if your fingers would just join in …'

It was a top-of-the-range Mercedes, a prize for Jason working so many hours that their children thought he was a stranger, and Shelley wasn't so sure if she knew him either. Sex was something they did on a Saturday night when CSI New York had finished. Dead on ten thirty, and usually over by ten forty-five. Always nice, for as long as it lasted. But not very fulfilling for either of them. She could hardly blame him. She was just as worn out as him, taking care of the children, so turning him on was sometimes just another chore. She hated herself for feeling that way about the man she still loved. So she'd made an extra-special effort this evening to turn herself back into the sexy siren he'd once known and loved. The silk gown she wore, over sexy lingerie, was a world away from the mumsy clothes she wore around the house. It made her feel reckless and just a little crazy. Now all she needed to do was make him crazy too so they could both forget the mortgage and the leaky tap in the bathroom and, just for a little while, that they were good old Mum and Dad.

Jason's fingers, no longer hesitant, trailed further up her thigh, pressing into her crotch, creating a delicious ache. She wriggled her hips against his fingers. 'Or,' she suggested, 'you could just throw me over the bonnet and fuck my brains out.' Jason gasped. It was a long time since she'd used language like that to him. It had the desired effect.

'That sounds like a plan.' His mouth was close to her ear, his fingers more urgent, sliding her dress upwards to reveal stocking-clad legs. He gently squeezed the skin between the suspenders in his thumb and forefinger. 'Do you know why I first asked you out?' he murmured against her neck.

'Because you were madly in love with me, I hope,' she said.

'Hmm, that too. But also because Billy told me you were the best pussy he'd ever had.' He continued pinching the flesh at the top of her legs, tantalisingly touching her panties with his fingers, then moving away. She slid down the seat a little, moving towards his touch. 'I had to try it for myself.' His breath tickled her neck. Turning her head to his, she kissed him, darting her tongue into his mouth. Her hands reached for his tie, pulling him further into her. She knew the game he wanted to play; it was an old favourite of theirs.

'Was he right?'

'Oh, God, yes. That's why I married you. I wanted it all to myself.' He reached her panties, which were already moist, massaging her through the silky fabric. 'He told me about the time he had you over his mother's dining table. How you scratched his back when you came. Then there was that time in his car, when you rode him on the back seat.' Shelley writhed beneath his touch, aroused by the memory and the fact that Billy and Jason had discussed her. It made her feel like a dirty girl and the feeling wasn't at all unpleasant.

Their kissing became deeper, tongues colliding and swirling together. Her knicker elastic cut into her as he slipped the gusset aside and parted her labia with one finger while another finger explored her, sliding into her, but not far enough. Her hips rose to meet him, and she became impatient with the underwear that stopped him from touching her as deeply as she wanted. She reached down and tore off her panties, crying out as they cut deeper. She stroked his cheek with the torn silk as he plunged two fingers into her, while his thumb moved in a circular motion on her clit. Her back arched towards him, her buttocks rising from the seat in intense ecstasy.

'Did Billy tell you I sucked him dry?' asked Shelley.

'Oh yes.'

Pulling at his belt, she unzipped his trousers, his bulging cock bursting out at her. She began by running her fingers along his length, lightly pinching the end, sliding her fingers back and forth, tugging at his foreskin. He groaned against her mouth, biting her bottom lip. His free hand went to her hair, pushing her face down. The damp tip of his prick touched her cheek. She lightly licked the top, swirling her tongue then poking it into the recess at the top, and then she took him whole into her mouth.

He groaned and tugged at her hair one moment, then pushed her head deeper the next, while his other hand reached beneath her and fondled her breast through her dress, pinching her nipple hard when his own excitement rose. He was close to completion when he stopped her, pulled her out of the car, and around to the front. It was icy cold outside, so when he pushed her back on the bonnet and pulled her legs apart the cold air that hit her vulva made her gasp, and she felt the moulded metal of the car press into her back. He stopped to look at her for a moment, as she glistened damp in the moonlight. He started with his fingers again, pushing deeper and deeper as she writhed in ecstasy, forgetting the cold. She watched him as he lowered his head to her, teasing her wildly by flicking his tongue on her clit in quick strokes, then pulling back, then starting again. She desperately wanted to grab his hand and ram his face into her, so his tongue went as far as his fingers, but when she tried, he deftly caught hold of her two hands with his one, and continued to torment her by only giving her a tiny taste of what she really wanted.

'Please, Jason, please,' she cried. 'All of it. I want it all.'

'Is that what you said to Billy when he licked your pussy?'

'Yes, yes.' She knew he was imagining her with Billy, her legs wide open while Billy tongued her till she exploded into his mouth. The image turned her on too. She hadn't thought of Billy for a long time, but he was just a teenage boy she'd once known. Jason was a man, and far more exciting. Not that she was willing to tell him that yet. The more jealous he was, the harder he tried to please her.

'And did he?'

'Yes!'

Finally he thrust his tongue into her while his fingers pulled her labia apart, giving her pain and pleasure, just the way he knew she liked it. She howled with pleasure as her first orgasm burst from her.

Jason stood up straight and wiped his lips with his fingers, smiling down at her. He pulled her to her feet, turned her around and lifted up her dress to reveal her bare buttocks. Without ceremony, he bent her over and thrust into her. Her bare nipples crushed against the metal bonnet, hardening more against the cold steel.

'Did Billy do this to you?'

'Yes,' she lied, and laughed when Jason thrust harder. The tops of her thighs were soaking wet, and the chill air enhanced the sticky, trampy feeling of her used body.

'Had you over the bonnet of a car?'

'Yes.'

'And others?'

Now he was imagining her with other men. Backs of cars, bus shelters, shop doorways, park benches and once on a dance floor, where she'd pulled the man in question into a corner and ridden him while pretending, not very convincingly, to be dancing.

'They told me about the things you'd do for them.' His hands reached around her and, sliding through the side of her low-cut top, cupped her breasts.

'Yes!'

'Sucking all that cock.'

'Yes!'

He groaned, his thighs slapping against hers.

'Yes,' she said. 'Yes.' Her head was spinning as the pressure started to build in her lower belly. She fought to hold back, not wanting the feeling to end, wanting to stay at that point. But he was more determined than her, moving faster and harder, tickling the spot deep inside her, making it burn, pulsate. She banged the car bonnet with her hands, trying to find something to hold on to as her excitement soared. She reached behind her awkwardly and caught one of his arms, digging her nails through his jacket as she screamed her completion. So intense was the sensation, Shelley saw flashing lights and felt the earth rumble beneath them.

'My slut!' he cried when he came a moment later. He fell against her back, gasping and laughing.

Shaking, they managed to get to their feet, where he held her in his arms and kissed her. Gently this time.

'*My* darling slut,' he whispered. She'd never told him how much of her past she'd made up just to turn him on. It didn't seem to matter to him. All that mattered was the pleasure they got from each other discussing it and recreating her wildest fantasies.

'Ahem ...' a strange voice said. Orange lights flashed on top of the breakdown truck, and the engine growled gently. Shelley realised it was that she'd seen and felt when she climaxed.

Shelley and Jason turned around and saw the tow truck driver, who appeared to be caught between embarrassment and excitement.

'Ah, you're here,' said Jason, with wonderful understatement. 'I think it's the carburettor.'

A Good Deal
by Roxanne Sinclair

Magda left her case just inside the door, kicked off her shoes and made her way across the room. She fell backwards and bounced on the double-sprung mattress of the king-size bed.

Staying in good hotels was one of the perks of her position in the company she worked for. It was the least that she deserved for spending twenty nights of every month on the road.

Here she was, another day in another town in another hotel. She thanked God that her PA, Patrick, kept her diary up-to-date because sometimes that was the only way that she knew where she was.

Magda smiled at the thought of Patrick. He was twenty-five years old, tall and muscular with his father's Scandinavian hair and his mother's Irish eyes.

She'd hired him with the hope of seducing him, but that was before she discovered that he was as gay as a summer's day.

It was a pity, but what the hell. He was great at his job and he was always good to look at on the rare occasions that she was in the office.

The mere thought of Patrick had started a tingle at the top of her legs. God, she needed a shag.

She showered for a long time, running her soapy hands over her wet body and enjoying the sensation.

When she dressed, she did so with one thing in mind in a dress that showed more cleavage and thigh than was appropriate for a woman on a business trip with an important meeting in the morning to prepare for.

When she left the bedroom, her morning meeting was the last thing on her mind.

As she walked into the bar her eyes swept over the four men who were seated around the room, and she felt the four pairs of eyes on her as she walked. She smiled, knowing that all of those eyes followed her while she walked all the way to the bar. She walked slowly to allow them plenty of time to appreciate her.

Magda perched herself on a stool and crossed her legs, allowing her skirt to ride up on her thigh. Her shoe fell loose as she rocked her foot, and she bent her toes to catch it.

'Can I help you?' the bartender asked with a smile.

Maybe later, Magda thought, but she said, 'White wine please.'

'Large?'

'Always,' Magda said, flirting outrageously.

'Let me get that.' The voice came from behind Magda. She looked over her shoulder and saw the man who had been sitting at the corner table.

'Thanks.'

Her new companion signalled that he would have the same again and the bartender poured vodka over two ice cubes.

He held the glass up: 'Cheers.'

Magda lifted her own glass by the stem and returned the salute. 'Cheers.'

'I'm Paul,' he said as he put his glass to his mouth.

'Pleased to meet you, Paul.' She took a mouthful of the cool Chardonnay and held it in her mouth for a few seconds before swallowing. 'I'm Margaret.' Well, she told herself, it's close enough. He didn't need to know her real name.

They made small talk for half an hour before Paul asked her to join him for dinner.

'I've got a table booked here,' he told her, 'but I could cancel that and go somewhere else if you'd rather.'

Magda smiled at the suggestion. That would come later.

'Here will be fine,' she said as she drained her glass.

'Then please be my guest.' He stood up and held out his hand to her.

She took his hand gently and allowed her skirt to ride up even further when she slid off the stool. She draped her hand on his shoulder to steady herself as she pushed her foot back into her shoe. He looked down and Magda knew that he was appreciating the shape of her leg as she played at putting the shoe back on.

As she pushed her skirt down, she leaned forward, allowing him a glimpse of the curve of her tits.

Sitting at the table under the subdued lighting of the restaurant, they eyed each other over the top of the menus that each of them held but neither of them was reading. At first they looked away from each other quickly, but after a few seconds they locked eyes.

Magda set her menu aside. What she wanted wasn't on that particular list.

'I'm your guest,' she said. 'I'll let you order for me.'

He gestured to the waiter and ordered the first thing he came to.

When the food was delivered, Magda caught the

waiter having a sly look down the front of her dress as he put the plate on the table. She smiled at him and he smiled back, not the least bit embarrassed by his indiscretion. He looked at her again as he placed Paul's food on the table.

'Thank you,' Paul said. He watched the waiter back away. 'I think you've got an admirer,' he commented, picking up his knife and fork. He stopped with the utensils poised for attack. 'Or should I say, another admirer.'

She looked down at her food to hide her smile.

She noticed that Paul ate his food quickly like he had somewhere to go, but she cut hers into tiny pieces and chewed each piece thoroughly. They both knew that they were heading for the same place, but while he couldn't wait to get there she found the anticipation stimulating.

But there was a stage as she dissected her salmon fillet when enough was enough. If she didn't get naked soon she was going to burst.

'Would you like anything else?' Paul asked as she placed her knife and fork together on the plate.

'Yes,' she replied, pushing the plate away.

'And what would that be?'

'You in room 447 in ten minutes.'

She got up and left Paul trying to attract the waiter's attention.

Once in the bedroom Magda slipped off her shoes and shrugged off her dress. It fell to her waist as she walked to the wardrobe, and she pushed it over her hips, allowing it to fall to the floor. She was bent over picking it up when she heard the knock on the door.

She laughed to herself as she grabbed the dress. 'Yes?' she called out seductively.

'It's Paul.'

She laughed again at the impatience in his voice and she took her time hanging the dress up before walking to the door wearing nothing but the lace G-string that she had worn under the dress.

She opened the door wide and without hesitation. She stood with her feet apart and her hands on her hips. He looked at her with a smile on his lips and an oak tree in his trousers.

'You came early,' Magda said, holding her hand out to him. She pulled him into the bedroom, 'Make sure it doesn't happen again.'

She closed the door and leaned against it.

'Are you ready for dessert?' she asked.

He looked her up and down before ripping off his clothes in record time. In less than a minute he stood before her more naked than she was with a pole that you could hang a flag from.

She tried not to show her appreciation of the size of his rod, which was a good eight or nine inches long. Experience had taught her that it wasn't what you had, it was what you did with it that mattered. She'd once had sex with a bloke in Cardiff whose cock wasn't much longer than her little finger but my god what he had done with it. Now, when she smiled, it was at the recollection of that night down by the docks, not by what was in front of her. She would reserve judgement on that until later.

Magda shimmied her way to the bed, wriggling out of her underwear as she did so. Then with a turn in mid-air she threw herself onto the mattress, which moved beneath her, causing her breasts to bounce wildly before settling.

She pushed herself on to her elbows and looked at Paul where he stood to attention just a few feet away.

'Well?' she asked.

'Well what?'

'What do you want to do now?'

'Whatever you want me to do.'

His smile created a sensation that told Magda that she was in for a good time.

She put her feet on the end of the bed and allowed her bent knees to fall to the side, lying exposed before him.

'I want you to pleasure me,' she told him.

That was all the invitation he needed and within seconds he knelt between her thighs. She laid back and massaged her nipples as Paul went to work on her pussy.

Magda wasn't sure what he was doing down there but she knew that she liked it. He used a mixture of fingers and tongue to knead and flick her towards ecstasy and she could both feel and hear the moisture rising in her hole.

In and out, in and out with first two fingers then three plunged deep inside her, his thumb catching her clit with each movement.

Her hips squirmed as her climax came and when her orgasm erupted through her body her hips thrust up towards his face. He took that opportunity to eat her cunt one more time. He poked his tongue deep into her hole and she tingled as he sucked out her juices.

'Dessert never tasted so good,' he told her.

She pushed herself back on to her elbows and looked at him framed between her bent knees.

'Fuck me,' she ordered playfully.

He pushed himself to his feet and stood over her. Then with the look of a man who knew he would perform well, he crawled on top of her, holding himself up with his hands.

With his face inches from hers he looked like he was going to say something but didn't. Instead he pushed himself away and Magda feared that he might have changed his mind. But she rested easy when he settled on to his knees and put his hands under her arse.

He lifted her up and latched her on to him with one swift practised movement.

Magda groaned as he filled her and waited for him to go to work. He rocked gently at first, barely even moving, then as he speeded up his thrusts became longer and deeper.

He flicked her ankles up and she locked her toes behind his neck. His hands went to her hips, pulling her onto him as he forced himself into her. With every bang his groin brushed her already excited clitoris and it wasn't long before she felt another explosion of pleasure.

Paul hadn't yet reached his own climax and in his effort to get there he increased the intensity of his movements.

And all the while Magda floated along on a wave of pleasure that made the night in Cardiff seem like a fumble behind the bike sheds.

When she felt him suddenly expand within her, stretching her wide beneath him, she knew that his moment was almost there and she screamed encouragement at him.

'Cream me,' she urged and sure enough he did.

They lay together for a long time. At first he was on top of her, taking the bulk of the weight on his elbows, and then they were side by side with the tangled sheets at their feet.

Eventually he said that he would have to go. He said that he had a big day ahead of him and he needed to get some sleep. He said that he had a meeting with a new supplier and he was hoping to screw a good deal out of them.

That would be when he'd find out that he already had and Magda would discover that Paul wasn't his real name either.

College Romance
by Sadie Wolf

She couldn't believe it when she'd been accepted into university. She'd never been one of the brightest kids, and then after leaving school she'd dropped out and worked in cafes and restaurants for three years before finally deciding she wanted to be a physiotherapist. She had got into her local university by going to night school and doing voluntary work to gain the required experience. Most of the students were younger than her, and a lot smarter. They were the straight-A students with the wealthy parents that she had been so in awe of at high school.

Throughout the first term, and beyond, she had the feeling that she shouldn't really be there: that at any moment someone was going to tap her on the shoulder and tell her there had been a mistake. She made up for feeling inadequate by working extra hard. She was the one who always did all the required reading, who always started her assignments and revision in good time. Her friends liked her because she was a good listener, and good at calming them down when they got stressed out over deadlines and exams.

Her private life was a bit of a mess. She had an on-off

relationship with a man who was more or less an alcoholic, although he would never have admitted to this. He would frequently disappear for several days after saying he was popping down the pub. When he was sober, he was warm and funny and kind, but drunk he was wild and unpredictable. On the whole, she kept him away from her university friends, and in any case, he was too unreliable to come to any of the nights out they arranged.

Most of the time, her hard work paid off, and although she still wasn't one of the high flyers, her grades were good. Then, in her second year, she suffered a crisis of confidence. Paul, the on-off boyfriend, had finally become 'off' for good, and she was feeling bereft and lonely. Her most recent assignment was returned with a D grade. She couldn't help it; she stood by the pigeonholes and cried.

It was quite common for students, especially the driven ones, to go and see the lecturer who had done the marking for some feedback about a bad grade. Maureen Fletcher was tough and plain speaking. She was respected and feared by the students. Donna knew there was nothing to be done about the assignment. She just wanted to know what exactly was wrong with it so it wouldn't happen again. Maureen's office was like all the others, a little frosted glass cubicle with a desk, computer and shelves of books and journals, except that she didn't have to share it with anyone like some of the more junior staff did.

'Sit down. There's nothing wrong with this other than the fact it's just not very well organised. I've marked your work before and it's usually a good, clear read, but this one was just a little chaotic. Here. It's not the end of the world.'

Tears had started falling down Donna's face in spite of her determination not to cry. She took the tissue that Maureen handed her. Once outside, she walked down to the end of the corridor and leant against the wall, trying to collect herself. She knew she was being silly, but she couldn't stop crying.

Stephen Williams was known for his strong attachment to acetates. Even after PowerPoint came into general use he still stuck with layering acetates one on top of the other, beginning with a plain outline and gradually building on it using different colours and copious arrows. Still, it worked. He taught neurology, and he had the gift of breaking down very difficult concepts and making them understandable. He wasn't flashy or theatrical, like some of the lecturers, who did things like pegging words on to giant washing lines rigged up across the lecture theatre; or handing out charity shop bras for them to categorise when they were learning about data collection.

Stephen told them stories about patients he had treated who had multiple sclerosis, strokes and Parkinson's disease. He explained how the nervous system worked, and what happened when things went wrong. He taught them to be grateful for the bodies they had, and they became aware of themselves in a way they hadn't been before. Every attack of pins and needles signified the start of multiple sclerosis, and a reminder of how lucky they were to have their health.

There was no getting around the fact that neurology was hard work. The students had to do their preparatory reading properly or they would be unable to keep up in class, and the subject required that they learn by heart which nerves supply which area of the body. Stephen rewarded their dedication by bringing the subject to life. More than just intellectually, he taught them how to understand how a sensation of temperature, pleasure or pain is experienced, talking them through what happens in the body and the brain when something touches the skin. Donna liked it best when he talked about feet and hands being tickled with feathers, and the sensation speeding along the nerves to the brain. It was then that she went all dreamy and faraway looking, and her friends began to tease her about having a crush on Stephen. Perhaps if no one had said anything, then nothing would have happened, but their comments made a vague sensation real and concrete.

Donna stood in the corridor, crying, torn between going home and going to find someone to talk to. She looked up as she heard footsteps in the corridor, and saw Stephen approaching her. *Shit, how embarrassing*, she thought, closely followed by, *but I want someone to talk to me, please let him stop!* He stopped in front of her, slightly awkward, wearing his trademark slightly crumpled shirt, chinos and trainers. He wasn't that much taller than her, slightly built, with a handsome, angular face and kind, grey eyes.

'Hey, Donna, what's up? Surely you haven't forgotten your moves for the synchronised swimming competition?' She laughed in spite of herself. It had become a standing joke that he referred to her as a synchronised swimmer, even though she had told him she only did regular swimming. 'Do you want to come and have a chat? I can rustle you up a cup of tea. No guarantee about the quality of it though.'

'OK. Thanks.' She followed him back down the corridor and into his office. His was exactly like Maureen's, only messier. There were piles of books and journals on the desk, and she noticed a folder overflowing with his trademark multicoloured acetates. He had a kettle on a tray in the corner of the room, and he filled it from a jug on the windowsill. She wondered, not for the first time, what it would be like to work at the university, purely concentrating on the accumulation of knowledge, and imparting that knowledge to the next generation. He handed her a mug of tea.

'So, what's up? Or is it private, boyfriend trouble?' He leant against his desk, facing her. She noticed how long his fingers were as he picked up his tea.

'No, nothing like that. I got a D in my last assignment, and I went to see Maureen and she told me I'd done what was required, I just hadn't written it very well.'

'Well, that hardly sounds like the end of the world.'

Donna laughed.

'That's exactly what she said.'

'Well there you go. Great minds think alike. You know, everyone has off days; we all do work that's not as good as we could sometimes. Even me.'

'Really?' She looked up at him, noticing the laughter lines around his eyes and mouth, wondering again how old he was.

'Really. We're not superhuman, you know. When I first started teaching here I was only one step ahead of the students most of the time. Neurology was never my strong subject at university, and my friends all laughed at me when they found out I'd got this job.'

'But –'

'Yes, I know, I've got the hang of it now; I've been doing this job for years. You see, I love the subject, and the more I learned about it, the more I began to understand it in my own way. In a personal way, if you like, rather than just as a collection of facts.'

'That's what I like about your classes, the way you make it real.'

'Why, thank you. But seriously, you can't let one disappointing grade upset you. You're learning new things all the time, working really hard, you're bound to get overwhelmed at times. But you're doing really well, certainly in my classes, and I hear good things from the other tutors about you too. Students who come in via non-traditional routes get a lot of respect from the staff. Not because it's harder for you, more that you bring different experiences with you.'

'Oh, that's nice, thank you.'

There was an awkward pause. She felt herself going red. He turned away, doing something to his computer, shutting it down. She suddenly felt very self-conscious, aware of what her friends would say if they could see her now. The horrible thought came into her mind that he might have picked up that she had a crush on him. But of course he couldn't have, or he wouldn't have invited her into his office. She knew that lecturers had to be really careful about that kind of thing nowadays.

She looked around his office, at the pinboards covered with letters and adverts for conferences. A small photo of two young children was pinned up in the corner of one of the boards. Married with kids. Of course. That made him even safer, really. He switched off the monitor and turned back to her.

'What made you want to become a physiotherapist?'

'My mum's friend worked as a physio, in burns and plastics. I always found it kind of fascinating, and scary at the same time, the idea of working with burns patients. Because of what they look like, and the pain, I suppose. I mean, that's just what got me started thinking about it, and the more I found out about physiotherapy, the more I thought it was right for me.' She didn't tell him that she had spent three years washing up because she didn't believe she was good enough to do anything else.

'Look, how are you getting home? I can give you a lift if you like.'

He stood up and started shuffling papers into his bag. 'Hey, if you're still interested in burns and plastics, I used to have a job in that area. It was before I came here, so it was a while ago, but I could probably point you in the right direction. I've got a lot of stuff on it at home too, photos and so on, part of a research project. If you wanted.'

'Really? That'd be great. You know, it sounds silly, but I'm still worried I'd get a bit freaked out, you know, especially if it was people's faces.'

'That's not silly, it's human nature. The first time you see someone with any kind of facial disfigurement is always a bit of a shock. You're going to want to look, and you need to do that. But it is amazing, how it happens. You know how we're always taught to see the person? Well, that's exactly what happens, you look past the disfigurement. And the number one thing my patients said was, what meant the most to them was just having someone who would look at them and talk to them without flinching.' He zipped up his bag and picked up his jacket. 'So, I mean it, you'd be welcome to come round and take a look at some of that stuff.' He laughed. 'Don't worry: you'll be perfectly safe. I'm taking more of a risk inviting you, seeing as how I'm probably breaking all sorts of protocols. Or I could just take you straight home. It's up to you.'

*   *   *

Stephen lived in a small terraced house on the other side of town to the university, the cheaper side, Donna realised. His house was a lot more untidy than his office. It wasn't dirty, simply cluttered with books and papers on every surface. The walls of the sitting room were lined with bookshelves, making the room even smaller, so it felt more like a study than a sitting room. There was a large print on the wall that looked out of place in a room this size, and another painting propped up against one of the bookshelves, waiting to be hung up. It looked like he hadn't moved in long ago. She realised with a jolt that no wife and kids lived here: this was definitely the house of a man who had been through a divorce.

He put a bottle of wine and two glasses on the coffee table, next to a large wooden box.

'What's this?'

'Things to test sensation. Have a look. It's got the reflex hammers and the pinpricks but it's got some other stuff in there too; everyday things, most of it, different textures and temperatures. Some stuff gets stuck in the freezer or warmed up in hot water.'

'Did you put all this together?'

'Yeah, I've been messing about with it for ages, hoping to sell it to a testing company for megabucks. Like thousands of others, probably.'

'This is good, have you done any proper testing of it yet?'

'Well, not properly yet, no, but it's good fun at dinner parties. Except for when it isn't.'

'What do you mean?'

'I did it on a friend's girlfriend once, found she had altered sensation all down one of her legs. I was amazed she was walking around without falling over.'

'What was wrong with her?'

'Well, it wasn't that bad. She'd had meningitis as a child, and that had been one of the side effects. It was just that the sensation loss either hadn't been properly picked up at the time, or it had been forgotten about. Either way, she'd done a fantastic job of compensating, but it could have been really dangerous, with regard to burns or accidents.'

He went over to one of the bookshelves and started searching through some folders. With his back to her, she could watch him unashamedly. She bit her bottom lip. *She was in Stephen's house, drinking his wine!* He pulled down a fat black lever arch file and handed to her. 'Here. This is my burns and plastics research project. I'm proud to say it formed part of a successful bid to increase the amount of physio for burns patients in that trust.'

'Well done.' She opened the folder and was confronted with a page of photographs of young burns patients, their red limbs contracted, horribly damaged.

'Shock tactics. What happens with no or inadequate physio. There are some happier pictures later on.' He refilled her glass.

Red wine always went straight to her head since she wasn't used to it. She turned the pages of the folder. There were pages of data about degrees of functional movement, case histories and then, as he had promised, happier photos. Kids who had still been terribly burned, but the scarring was a lot flatter, and their limbs were far less contracted, in more normal positions. It really was very good work, and to think it had actually meant that more kids had been properly helped … She felt her eyes begin to sting. Oh for heaven's sake. She put the folder down.

'Can I use your loo?'

She sat on the loo and tried to clear her head. She'd had two glasses of wine, but she felt quite drunk. She remembered that in all the upset of the day she hadn't had any lunch. That explained it. She was in the *house* of her lecturer, the one she had a big crush on. He was quite clearly post divorce, or at least post separation, but she didn't believe he'd brought her back in order to put the moves on her. If anything were going to happen, she'd have to give him a helping hand. She couldn't believe what she was thinking: he could lose his job, he'd be mad to do it. But it did happen though, didn't it? Just before she started university she'd read an article in the NME giving a list of must-try student experiences. It had been aimed at kids coming straight from home, but the one about having sex with a tutor had stuck in her mind. She slipped off her tights, rolled them up and put them in her handbag. She looked at herself in the mirror: smudged mascara, tied-back hair, no lipstick. She cleaned up her mascara, untied her hair and brushed it out. Worn loose, her hair was quite long, shoulder length, a lovely glossy brunette colour. She put on some pink lip-gloss. She smiled at herself in the mirror: much better.

He was sitting on the sofa, fiddling with the wine bottle. She sat down next to him, and picked up the wooden box.

'Will you do me? I haven't got anything wrong with me, I promise. And my feet are clean.' She slipped off her shoes and wiggled her toes. He toenails were painted bright pink.

'I don't know, Donna.'

She pulled her skirt up over her knees.

'Please. It's OK. I want you to.'

151

He ran his fingers through his hair and stared at the carpet. She put a hand on his arm.

'Please.' She held her breath.

'OK.'

He rolled up his sleeves, took the box from her hands and knelt down beside her. 'Right, lie down and close your eyes.' He started with the balls of her feet and worked his way steadily upwards. She had to rate each different sensation, and compare left and right. The pinpricks hurt a little, and the cold tickled, but that was all. She liked the way his fingertips trembled slightly as he applied the tester to her skin, and she liked the way her skin came alive when it was touched. When he reached her knees, he stopped.

'Well, you're perfectly intact so far, neurologically speaking. Um, that's usually as far as I'd go at a dinner party.' His voice sounded strange. He laughed nervously.

She raised herself up on one elbow and looked at him.

'But we're not having a dinner party, are we? I thought I was the patient. And I'd like you to check *all* of my legs, if you don't mind.' She pulled her skirt a little higher.

'Donna –'

'It's OK.' She took hold of his hand and laid it on her thigh. She thought for a moment that he was going to pull away, but then she felt him give in, and she lay back down again and closed her eyes.

The box was abandoned now: it was his fingertips tracing up and down the inside of her thighs, sending electricity shooting up and down her body. She felt her skin tingle and heat up under his hands, and in her mind she begged him to go higher. She hardly dared to move, let alone speak, in case he changed his mind, came to his

152

senses and stopped. She felt that she would die of frustration if he stopped. Everything she had dreamed of, when he was talking in class about stroking skin with the lightest of touches, and that touch being transmitted, and when she had imagined him doing it to her, all that was happening now, and she didn't want anything to break the spell.

After what felt like forever, his fingertips began to trace the edges of her knickers, and then slipped inside the material, tracing the crease at the top of her thigh, teasing her. He slipped his hands underneath her bottom and pulled down her knickers, then parted her thighs with his hands. He rested his head on her thigh for a moment, kissed her lightly, then buried his face between her legs, slipping his tongue inside her and then upwards, licking her clit with gentle, steady strokes. She could feel his warm breath on her and the wetness that had spread to her thighs cooling in the air. She wrapped her arms around his shoulders and stroked his hair, enjoying the feeling of his head moving up and down under her hands. He slipped his fingers inside her, adding more until it was almost painful, moving in and out of her firmly and steadily. She felt as though he was going to make her come soon, and he must have felt it too, because he pulled away and quickly undid his trousers and pulled them off, and climbed naked on to her. He guided his cock in with his hand, and put a hand under her hips to move her closer to him. With their bodies pressed together perfectly, he fucked her slowly and steadily, until she felt herself building towards a climax again, and then he pressed himself harder into her, moving against her in small circles, so she came suddenly, crying out. He let himself climax then, and she felt his cock pulsing inside her as the last spasms of her orgasm died down.

Afterwards, he drove her home, and although neither of them said anything, she knew it would never happen again. It was a once-in-a-lifetime opportunity, and even if she'd had to behave like a cheap tart to make it happen, she was glad that it had.

Clean-up Duty
by Karyn Winter

'You're not even touching her and she's trembling.'

I try to move my head in the direction of her voice, but a hand in my hair holds me back. I remain still, straining to get a mental image of what is happening beyond the darkness.

'She's trembling because she knows what's going to happen. Or she thinks she does.'

He's right behind me, his voice loud in my ear, although I didn't hear him move. His warm breath tickles my neck as he speaks, making me tremble harder despite my best efforts not to. He chuckles.

'You see, right now, she's nervous but also excited. The erect nipples' – at that, a hand twists my piercing and I bite back a moan – 'give that away. She's on the back foot though. When you can't see what's happening your imagination just runs away with you. Which can be exciting or terrifying. Or both.'

I can almost see his malevolent smile through the blindfold. The smile guaranteed to make me simultaneously wet between my legs and nervous in the pit of my stomach.

I hear movement. Rustling. Clothes possibly. Maybe he's naked now. Maybe she is. My teeth are gritted with frustration at not being able to see them. I can feel they're close, and now I'm hearing them kiss; she exhales a gentle murmur of pleasure as they break apart.

I stand compliant, exactly as I have been left, arms behind my back, crossed at the wrists, a textbook submissive pose. I don't know exactly how this is going to play out but I am not doing anything to risk not playing a full part in it.

'Are you feeling left out?'

As he speaks, a tentative tongue licks my breast. Circling, circling and then, finally, suckling me into wet warmth. The sensation is heightened by the fact I can't see her, can just smell her perfume and feel her tongue rolling around my nipple, lapping at me, tasting me for the first time. I imagine what she must look like, her gorgeous mouth clamped round my tit, her full lips suckling me. But as the mental image begins to form I am shocked out of it.

His mouth round my other nipple is harder. He sucks me in a way that makes me squirm. Where she is soft he is vicious, his teeth scraping the delicate flesh, his fingers pinching into my breast as the pressure increases to the point where I feel like I'm going to cry out. The two different sensations merge together, a mixture of pain and pleasure intrinsically connected. Blurred. Scared to cry out, I close my eyes to stop tears soaking the cloth of the blindfold. But he sucks harder, bites harder until the sound is forced from the back of my throat, shattering the silence of the room.

He stops. They both stop. Although she plants a tender kiss on my nipple before moving away.

Even in the darkness I can feel them looking at me, and suddenly get a flash of how I must look, naked, blindfolded, obviously aroused. I feel myself blushing.

'We've had to stop because she made a noise. She's not supposed to make a sound. Unfortunately she often does things she's not supposed to do.'

He moves closer to me, runs a finger along my collarbone, pushing away a stray tendril of hair. 'What do we do when you do things you're not supposed to do?'

I close my eyes behind the blindfold, feeling the blush deepen. I know what he wants me to say and I know what'll happen if I don't say it. But a small part of me still hates to form the words. The dual submission – not just to him but to the part of me that wants this, needs this, gets turned on by the humiliation of it – sticks in my throat.

As I try to gather my thoughts he slaps my breast, the sound echoing across the room. 'Too slow. Answer me. Tell her what happens.'

For the first time since he put the blindfold on I am thankful that it's there, that they can't see the truth in my eyes. My answer is quiet, I need to clear my throat before I can speak.

'You punish me.'

His hand twists in my hair. He moves it, a tug of warning. 'I didn't hear you.'

Louder: 'You punish me.'

His voice is steel cased in velvet. 'That's right. How do I punish you?'

My temper is rising – he bloody knows how he punishes me because he's the one who does it, and he's only making me say it out loud because he knows it makes me embarrassed. I am angry and I am wet and the fact I can feel myself getting wetter as I stand in front of them only makes me more furious.

I try to hide the annoyance but I can hear the

157

sharpness in my tone. 'It depends. Whip. Belt. Cane. Crop. Hand. Whatever pleases you when you do it.'

I hear the sound of leather slipping through belt loops and my heart starts pounding. I am manoeuvred across the floor and shoved unceremoniously onto my hands and knees on the bed. My bearings are lost and I can't picture where I am in the room. I try to adjust my position so I feel slightly less precarious, but as I shuffle vulnerably in the darkness, trying to feel my way so I don't topple off the bed, I don't have time to prepare for the first blow.

He explains to her how he is hitting me. The best way to hold the belt. The angle to take. How to mix between hitting places you've hit before and new places so you can watch the reaction to the different kinds of pain. When to hold back. When to push harder.

The pauses make it difficult to process the pain as there's no rhythm to it, no way of riding the peaks and troughs. Instead I retreat into it, only half aware of their discussion about the welts on my arse and how long they will take to go down as I listen intently for the whistle of the belt through the air to try to prepare myself for the next wave of pain.

I don't know how long it goes on but finally there is blessed respite. Four hands run over the marks, her fingernails tracing the lines marking the path of the belt, he brutally squeezing the most punished curve of my arse until I whimper. Then, for the most fleeting moment, so gently that I wonder whether I'm imagining it, a finger runs up my slit. I moan in frustration as it moves away.

Her voice is filled with a quiet wonder. 'This is making her wet.'

I can hear her wetness as he touches her. She sighs in

pleasure. 'It's making you wet too.' His voice is pleased. Her laugh is breathy and a little nervous and somehow her uncertainty makes me feel reassured.

A finger touches my lips; I open and suck it deep, licking her nectar from his finger. He laughs at my enthusiasm. 'She's very keen. Do you want a go?'

The reassurance disappears in a puff of smoke. Arousal has dulled my brain. Does he mean does she want a go at tasting me? Licking him? Or does he seriously mean to …

The hiss of the belt through the air is so quick I have no time to prepare. I can't help but scream as not only is her swing hard but she catches me in the tender spot where my arse meets the top of my thigh. I am gasping through the pain, tears in my eyes as I try to regain my position.

His voice is amused, calm. 'From that angle you don't need that much swing. If you do it that hard then you're going to break the skin. Try again.' I am quivering in terror, waiting for her next move. The longer the silence stretches the more every nerve ending of my body moves towards breaking point. When she does hit me I bite my lip to try to withstand the impact, the taste of blood metallic in my mouth. I withstand her blows, which are lighter than the first touch but still leave me fighting the urge to squirm away. My blood is singing in my ears by the time I finally hear the belt hit the floor and the bed move.

She moans as he enters her. The bed starts to rock with his thrusts, the scent of her arousal and the wet sound of their fucking betraying how much she's enjoying this game. I stay in position, wishing I could see the picture they make, just a few inches away from me, through the black satin of the blindfold. A slap on my arse brings me back to the moment, cruel fingers grabbing me by the hip and pulling me up the bed, closer to them.

'Lie down on your back.'

Gingerly I lie down, trying to avoid putting undue pressure on the welts forming on my arse, already stinging at the abrasive cotton sheet.

'Well? Make yourself useful.'

His voice is pretty much directly above me, but I'm unsure what he wants me to do. Suddenly the blindfold is ripped from my face, and I blink at the sudden brightness, while my eyes adjust to what is in front of me. They are joined together just inches from my mouth. It's one of the horniest things I've ever seen.

'Well, come on. We're not waiting forever. You know what to do.'

I scoot up, eager, the chafing of my arse forgotten in my haste to fasten my mouth round her clit. I begin to lick her, his balls against my cheek as I run my tongue up and down her cunt lips. He starts to move and I stop to enjoy the view, before a sharp tweak of the nipple reminds me of my place. I watch his cock, slick with her juice, pound in and out of her, lapping at both of them as they fuck each other senseless in front of my face.

I can't resist watching her expression as she comes. She is beautiful. Watching the various emotions flash across her face and then seeing the moment where she loses any sense of herself or where she is makes my cunt clench in sympathy. I think he feels the same, as her moans have barely quietened before he starts to make the guttural moans of his orgasm. I watch him pump into her, see the trail of spunk still dripping from his cock as he pulls out, grabs my hair and pushes me face first into her pussy.

160

I have spent so long wondering what she'd taste like, and finally I get to find out. I push my tongue up inside her eagerly, kissing her cunt the way I'd like to kiss her mouth. She clenches around me, her hands tangling in my hair, pushing me further until all I can taste and smell is her, my face covered in her juice. She is writhing against me, grinding her clit against my face as she gets more excited.

He pushes a couple of fingers deep into my wetness and I moan into her cunt, which makes her moan too. But all too briefly the moment has passed and he's gone. I whimper in frustration, but before the sound has left my throat, he's pushing his fingers, slick with my own juices, into my arse. He works the wetness around my hole, lubing me up, making me moan before he pushes his fingers back high into my cunt. I push back against him, eager to be fucked this way, any way actually, I am so desperate for my release. I catch my arse on his elbow in my haste and gasp in pain – the swift exhalation of my breath into her cunt making her moan even more. I am trying to focus on the gorgeous woman whose legs I am between, but with the welts of my arse, the fingers pushing insistently up inside me and how desperately horny I have become having seen them fuck, it's very difficult, even with her gorgeous pussy in my face. Especially when I feel him pushing his cock into my arse. Even while I want his cock in me I can't stop myself, it is too big, and involuntarily I clench around him, denying him entry. He slaps me hard across the bum and in the split second I gasp and react to the pain he has pushed past my defence until he is firmly inside me, his hands resting on my still-warm arse cheeks.

I think she has looked up and seen me impaled on his cock, because suddenly she is moaning more and grinding herself against my face like she is ready to come again. My jaw is aching, but the thought of her coming around my tongue makes me lick her harder despite the fact I already feel like I'm drowning in her juice. As he starts to move inside me, he pushes my rabbit vibrator into my cunt and switches it on. The sensations, one on top of the other as he begins to move in and out of my arse are just too much to bear. It's like an assault on all my senses. The vibrations move through me, and I come loudly, my screams of pleasure swallowed up by her cunt.

Some women love multiple orgasms. Don't get me wrong, I do if I'm given some recovery time between them. Who's going to look a gift horse in the mouth? But in the few minutes after I come I am so sensitive that being touched is almost painful. As I gasp for breath, trying to regain my composure from the force of my orgasm, he switches the vibrator up higher and pushes it further inside me until I feel like I'm going to be split apart being fucked in both holes at once. I am whimpering, trying to form words of entreaty to beg him to give me a moment, eventually just crying out with the force of it all.

By the time he deigns to finish with me I am about to pass out from the orgasms wrung out of my battered and bruised body. I have no sense of time. I just want to crawl away because the sensation is so intense it's actually painful – yes, I know pain from excessive pleasure, very puritanical of me. But the more he rides me and the more he fucks me with the toy, the more fun she's having and so it goes on – until by the end I'm just a mess, covered in my own and everyone else's juices and wanting to sleep for a week.

Of course I don't get a chance to sleep like that, the

occupational hazard of being the lowest of the low in a BDSM sandwich I guess. The night was a long one, and I felt the after-effects of it for weeks afterwards. I also still have rude dreams about it sometimes, which I guess is understandable for one of the sexiest experiences of my life. I don't know that it'll ever happen again, but I can honestly say it's the most fun I've ever had on clean-up duty.

Sparkie's Wild Night
by Red

Red sighed as she closed the door to the kids' bedroom. Asleep at last! It had been such a long day. She smiled to herself thinking of the evening ahead. Sparkie wasn't due home from work for about three-quarters of an hour, so she still had time to prepare. The smile spread further as she pictured his face. Yes, she was sure he'd like her surprise. She certainly hoped he would.

After picking up the last of the kids' toys, Red went to the bathroom and turned on the shower. The room filled with steam and Red slowly removed her clothes, watching herself in the mirror, imagining she was stripping just for Sparkie. She gently teased down her hipsters, leaving them round her thighs, and smiled at her reflection in the mirror. She stroked her hands over her bum, giving her cheeks a little squeeze, just the way Sparkie would. She loved the feel of his hands on her flesh. He made her feel alive. The thought of him led her hand to her soft pink lacy knickers. She slid her hand down the front and parted her warm pussy, allowing two fingers to gently slip inside her. 'Mmm,' she sighed, wishing it was Sparkie with his hand down there right now. She removed her hand and breathed in the smell of her wet fingers. She smelt sweet tonight and tasted great too, she thought, as she sucked each of her fingers in turn.

Red removed the rest of her clothes, climbed into the shower and stood under the hot stream of water. The warmth of the water made her feel so relaxed and washed away the stresses of the day as it sprayed onto the back of her neck. She picked up the soap and stroked the soft lather over her breasts and down her thighs. Thoughts of Sparkie filled her head. It would be so nice to have him standing here in front of her now; she'd stand behind him, kiss his neck and hold him close, run her soapy hands over his chest and down his stomach, stroke the insides of his thighs and gently caress his cock and balls. Red smiled to herself ... not long now and he'd be home. She climbed out of the shower and rubbed her skin softly with her towel.

Her things were laid out on the bed already. 'Will he be up for this tonight?' she wondered. 'Of course he will. Do bears shit in the woods? He'll love it,' she chuckled to herself.

She pulled on the short black latex dress; she'd bought it just the other day online. It was like the one she'd had before, only sexier. A little surprise for Sparkie! The dress clung to her body like an extra skin, pushing her breasts up and together. She sat on the edge of the bed and slid her lacy-topped stockings slowly onto her feet, easing them up her legs into position. A tiny black G-string only just covered where it touched.

'Heels or boots,' she thought to herself. 'Boots.' The knee-high, zipped ones that held her legs tight and made them look sleek and sexy. He'd love those. She brushed her hair loose over her shoulders, put on some lippy and stood in front of the mirror. She wanted to look just right for him ... yes, that should do it.

165

Red made her way to the kitchen, praying that no one would knock on the door while she was dressed up like this. 'Sure-fire way of getting shot of a door-to-door salesman!' she laughed to herself.

She had lots of goodies in the fridge, ice in the ice tray, some milk chocolate fingers, fresh cream, strawberries. A veritable feast! Everything was ready in the lounge too, cushions, blankets, a wooden chair and her bag of tricks. Once she'd checked everything was just so, Red sat on the arm of the chair by the front door and waited.

She didn't have to wait long before she heard Sparkie's key in the front door. She braced herself, filled with excitement and nervousness.

Sparkie walked into the room, his face spreading into a huge grin as he saw Red.

'New dress, sweetheart?' he beamed at her. 'Nice, very nice.'

Red said nothing and pressed her body into his, her arms around his neck. She breathed him in. 'That's better,' she thought. 'He's home.'

Red sprawled herself along the sofa, one knee bent. 'Get undressed,' she barked with a cheeky grin.

Sparkie didn't complain; he began tearing at his shirt and scrabbling out of his trousers. In no time he was naked, standing in front of Red, hands on his hips, trying to look masterful.

'On your knees,' Red pointed to the floor in front of her. 'Just here, so I can reach you.' Sparkie did as was asked of him. He loved this game. Red got to her feet and began walking round Sparkie in circles. 'Don't look at me,' she snapped. 'Look at the floor.' He bowed his head and Red walked round to his arse. Reaching into her bag she pulled out a riding crop. 'I've bought you another little surprise, baby,' she teased. 'No peeping now.' The crop let out a crack as it made contact with Sparkie's arse. He winced and arched his back, wanting more. Red began tapping the end of the crop in her hand and started to walk round and round Sparkie again. She stroked the length of his spine and teased between his arse cheeks and his balls with the leather of the crop. Then, she flicked it back and down over his backside. He moaned quietly with both pleasure and pain, nervously anticipating the next strike. His cock was huge and hard now. He loved it when Red took control. He didn't want her like that all the time. There were times when he'd throw her roughly on the bed and take her hard, but for now he was her little toy. He would do just as she pleased.

Red slid her hands through Sparkie's hair, letting it run through her fingers. She stroked his head and neck again and again then suddenly locked her fingers, holding his hair firmly in her hand. Not pulling hard, just restraining. She stood against the wall in front of him, pulling his head towards her to make him follow; she slipped her G-string to one side and noticed just how damp it was already. She was so horny for him. Red pulled Sparkie's face into her wet pussy, holding him tight against her. His tongue was hot and wet and he lapped at Red's swollen lips and clit. 'Deeper,' she moaned, flicking repeatedly at his arse with the crop. Sparkie did as he was told and pushed his tongue in harder and deeper, fucking her with his tongue, making her want him all the more, but she was in control. She'd make him wait. Red released Sparkie's hair and stroked his face then roughly pushed him away, pulled off her G-string and strode over to sit open legged on the sofa, leaving Sparkie on his knees.

Sparkie crawled on his knees and crouched between Red's open thighs. 'Let me eat your pussy, Red,' he pleaded.

'No,' she smirked. 'You can just sit there and watch.'

Red began to masturbate herself, rubbing continually round the outside of her pussy in small circles, gently letting her fingers just flick her clit as they passed, stopping to slip a finger or two inside her, then holding her sweet-smelling fingers under Sparkie's nose and sliding them into his mouth.

'Please, baby, let me taste your pussy. You smell great.'

Red grinned cheekily and bent forward to kiss him, long and hard on the lips. 'OK baby.'

Red lay back and spread her pussy lips wide open with her fingers, her flesh pink and distended. Sparkie probed deep inside with his tongue, flicking it round her protruding clit, then sucking and licking at each of her fleshy lips in turn. His eyes sparkled. Red cried out and lifted her legs high, pressing her boot-clad feet into Sparkie's bare shoulders. She pushed hard with her legs, kicking him and play-fighting him off. Sparkie fought back, stretching his neck and struggling to nuzzle his face back into Red's pussy. Red flicked out with the crop across Sparkie's back. She noticed the whip marks on his arse and back, and the prints of her boot heels in his shoulders, and smiled. Sparkie was smiling too.

'Enough,' said Red, kicking Sparkie away. She got to her feet and rummaged in her bag of tricks. 'Just something to stop you being nosy,' she giggled. Red pulled out their blindfold and slipped it over Sparkie's eyes, plunging him into darkness and dragging him into fantasy. Leaving him on his knees and in the dark, Red disappeared into the kitchen.

Sparkie knew she had gone; the noise of her boots on the wooden floor gave her away ... The question was, 'What next?' His cock swelled at the thought of what she may do to him. He could hear her clanking about in the kitchen and then clomping through the house; the sound of her footsteps getting closer made him hornier. Red was standing next to him now; he could sense her presence.

Red slipped a strawberry into Sparkie's mouth. 'Mmm,' he said, expecting much worse than a food-tasting session. 'They're nice.' Suddenly, there was a burning sensation on his back, or was that cold? No, it was bloody freezing. Sparkie shivered as Red slid an ice cube over his flesh; the cube began melting and ice-cold water trickled down over his anus, making him tighten it. Red danced the rapidly disappearing cube down the length of Sparkie's spine, over his arse and just below his balls. Sparkie drew his stomach in and moaned as his balls shrank back away from the cold. It felt so horny. Red flicked at his arse hard with the crop and walked away from him.

Taking a chocolate finger from the pack, Red slid it into her pussy. She left it there for just a few minutes, and then gently slid it in and out of her, leaving the chocolate behind inside her; then she teased the biscuit against Sparkie's lips and into his mouth. Red reached for the tub of cream and pulled the top of her dress forward, just far enough to allow her to tip the ice-cold cream down inside. The latex held the cream against her skin, making her gasp. It slowly began to trickle down her stomach, and she rubbed the outside of the latex dress, slipping and sliding the cream over her breasts and into her pussy. Red stood in front of Sparkie, cream running down between her legs and dripping onto the floor. She held his hair firmly in her fingers once more and pulled his mouth towards her hot and now sticky pussy. Sparkie loved eating Red's pussy, but he was getting more than he'd bargained for this time. Red closed her eyes and moaned as Sparkie lapped hungrily at her swollen mound, licking her clean, inside and out. 'Mmm,' he sighed, licking his lips.

'Stand up,' Red commanded. She dragged the wooden chair across the floor and helped Sparkie to sit down. 'Put your hands behind the chair.' Sparkie did as he was told and Red slid his wrists into their handcuffs. She bound each of his legs tightly with ropes to the legs of the chair and sat facing him, straddling his lap. Red began biting Sparkie's erect nipples. She licked each one slowly then blew gently on it to make it stick out before nipping it hard, making Sparkie hold his breath and gasp with pleasure and pain.

Gripping tightly to Sparkie's huge beast of a cock, Red slid it up inside her dress. The latex held it tight against her and she could feel it throbbing and hard on her belly. Picking up the cream, Red poured a little more down the front of her dress. The cream trickled down onto Sparkie's cock and he drew breath sharply. Red slid her hand up and down his cock from the outside of the dress; the cream made the latex slippery and it felt so sexy and Red was being driven wild for him.

'I want you,' breathed Sparkie into Red's neck.

'If you want it, you gotta take it,' laughed Red. Sparkie struggled in his binds. He tilted his waist back and forth, desperately trying to slip his cock into Red's hot pussy. Red teased him, squatting over the end of his cock, letting it just part her lips, ever so slightly, then lifting herself up out of reach. She then teased him again. Sparkie was becoming wild. He so wanted to bang his cock hard into Red's pussy. She wanted it too. She bit hard into Sparkie's neck and slid herself fully onto his cock. He felt fantastic inside her, huge and throbbing. She held tight on to Sparkie's shoulders and slowly squatted up and down on his cock, feeling its full length. Then harder and faster, slapping her arse onto his lap. Sparkie was getting close to coming; she could feel his cock becoming hard, so hard that she moaned with pleasure and pain. Red pulled off the blindfold; she wanted to see Sparkie's eyes when he came, that wild look of being totally lost in her. She ground her pussy hard into him, again until her breasts almost bounced out of the top of the dress. Sparkie's eyes were wild and he opened his mouth as if to scream out. His body shook and Red could feel his hot cum squirting deep inside her, making her pussy grip tighter on to his cock and sending her over the edge into a frenzy of her own. She shuddered hard, her orgasm prolonging his, making them both cry out. Red flopped onto Sparkie's chest, hot and panting. She kissed his neck and licked a splash of cream from his face. Sparkie grinned – that grin, the one that needed no words.

Red smiled, 'Evening babe. Had a good day at work?'

A Brief Encounter
by Teddy Masters

The train rocks as it pulls away from the station. I stumble occasionally as I move down the corridor towards the first class carriage, looking for my seat. I find the compartment, slide open the door and walk in. I smile at the other occupant of the compartment, a woman with long brunette hair, hazel eyes and a beautiful smile ... you ...

I turn and place my case up in the racking and can almost feel your eyes burning into my back ... I turn again and that smile dazzles ...

I slide into my seat opposite you, the table between us holding your bag and a book ... my foot brushes yours as I shuffle towards the window. I apologise but you brush it aside with a quiet voice, a slight accent ... not American, Canadian I think ... 'Don't worry,' you say and smile again ...

I settle back in my seat, look out of the window but soon get bored. I turn my head to find you looking at me, a faint smile on your full red lips ... I get the feeling you don't mind me looking back at you and I smile too, my blue-grey eyes travelling slowly down from your brown ones, down over your nose, your lips, down over the curls of hair hanging lightly around your shoulders ...

You're wearing what looks like a cashmere dress, brown, a wrap style (Diane von Furstenberg maybe ...), simple, classy, elegant lines, the wrap as it crosses your chest emphasising what seems to be a deep and firm cleavage, your breasts carried high on your chest ...

My eyes travel back up and meet yours again ... you seem amused by my appraisal, but not offended, and a mischievous hint of a smile seems just to curl the corner of your mouth ...

The train rocks again, lurches, and your bag tips over on the table, spilling some of the contents on the surface, a few items scattering and a couple falling off the edge, onto the floor and rolling under my legs ... 'Let me,' I say as I slide from my seat ... I crouch down, thanking the train driver mentally for my opportunity to continue my visual discovery of you and your clothes ...

My hand gropes, blindly, for the items that fell to the floor and my eyes can't help but be drawn to the sight of that dress, stretched tightly over firm, shapely thighs and just down over your knees ... or be drawn to the sight of your legs emerging from under the brown cashmere, encased in very pale beige nylon ... or is it silk ...? It glistens as your legs move so, yes, silk I think ... elegant calves, neat ankles and feet in pale brown heels ... my eyes are transfixed as you lean over to see if I am having any luck retrieving your property, and as you lean over your legs move slightly and my eyes are drawn to a hint of lace halfway up your thigh as the wrap parts slightly ... you're wearing stockings ... oh god ...

My fingers finally close on your belongings ... one, two, three items ... I gather them together, tearing my eyes from your legs, and straighten up again, holding the things out to you and my fingers unfold ... opening my palm ... my eyes meet yours, yours open slightly wider, your lips part and that faint mischievous smile plays over them again as you see what I've picked up ... I drop my eyes down to my hand and my eyes widen as I see a tube of scarlet lipstick, a bottle of pink nail varnish ... and what looks like another lipstick, except for the tiny knurled base and the shiny, gold body ... and I realise what I am holding and pass it over quickly, smiling almost guiltily at you ... Your lips part again and your tongue just flickers lightly over them, that smile again ... You laugh and say, 'Thank you, I'll be needing those in a while.' My eyes widen further as I realise what you said ...

You replace your things in your bag and make a small show of doing the clasp up this time, before settling the bag on the seat beside you. I see you shift slightly in your seat, feel your leg brush mine and your eyes gaze at me ...

It seems as though you have returned your attention to your book and I look through the window at the scenery rushing by, the open Suffolk fields, the hedges, the rivers and dykes ... I hear a faint knock on the floor, my ears wondering what that could be ... Had I missed something when I was looking for your things earlier ...? Then I feel it, the unmistakable trace of a soft toe grazing my calf as it probes beneath the hem of my trousers ... I look at you again, that smile still playing on your lips and that mischief definitely flickering in your eyes ... The knock must have been you slipping your shoe off and now I can feel your foot slide back out from under my trouser leg and start to run softly up the outside of my leg, climbing higher, then retreating down ...

I shift slightly in my seat, moving my legs apart slightly as I feel that foot run softly up my right leg and see you slip gently down in your seat, bringing you closer to me ... Our eyes meet again and we hold each other's gaze ... I feel your foot moving higher, touching my thigh and I slip my hand under the edge of the table... My fingers find your foot, definitely silk stockings, and I trace my fingers over and around your toes as the ball of your foot presses against my thigh ...

I look at you again, your breath seems to be quickening and I see your breasts heaving softly inside the cashmere ... As you twist slightly and lean, the wrap parts a little and I catch a glimpse of a pale cream lace bra, intricately detailed, and a firm, smooth, lightly tanned breast softly encased within it ...

Your foot presses higher and firmer against my leg, my fingers slide over your ankle and up your calf, the smooth silk ruffling softly under my palm ... Then, suddenly, abruptly, your foot is withdrawn and I hear, sense, you slipping your toes back into your shoe ... I look at you, surprised, but that smile is still there and you lean forward and whisper softly, 'I need to go to the loo ...,' and you slip out from under the table and stand, straightening your dress with your back to ,raps of your suspenders under the smooth brown material of your dress. You pick up your bag, move towards the door, slide it open, step through and then, as if an afterthought, half turn back to me and say, 'Follow me, in a couple of minutes. Knock once, wait a second, then knock twice and I'll know it's you.' And then you're gone, turning right, and your heels clip softly down the corridor towards the end of the carriage ...

My mind whirls ... did I actually hear you say that ...

I wait, my heart beating fast, the adrenaline coursing through me. I shift in my seat, uncomfortable now with the growing bulge in my trousers ... I look at my watch, one minute gone ... I watch the second hand tick slowly round and eventually meet the hour marker ...

I make up my mind ... I slide from behind the table, stand and walk to the door which you had left open ... I leave the compartment and turn right too ... tracing your steps along the corridor till I reach the compartment at the end. Thank God these new trains have better facilities I think as I look at the door, closed and with the occupied sign showing ...

I take a deep breath, knock once, wait briefly, then tap again, twice, softly. I hear the latch being drawn immediately and the door click open ... I look around, push the door slightly and step in ...

The cubicle is larger than I remember from my youth... a good job too as I look across to you, leaning back against the sink, your bag hanging from the peg beside you. 'Um, hi,' I begin but you lean forward slightly, take my hand in yours and pull me gently towards you. As I near you, you tilt your head up slightly, parting your lips, and I lean down and our lips meet ... your soft, sweet warm breath flowing over my lips. I feel your tongue flicker softly at the corner of my mouth and I feel you lift my hand up and press my palm against your breast ... and even through the soft cashmere of your dress and the delicate lace of your bra I can feel your nipple, hard, jutting, poking into the palm of my hand. I flex my fingers, stiffening my hand, forcing it firmly against you ... you catch your breath and I kiss your mouth more firmly, pressing our lips together ... Caressing your breast with my hand, I slide it inside the fold of your dress ... warm flesh under my fingertips ...

Your hand snakes round the back of my neck as you pull me closer ... we kiss, we lick each other's lips and

176

tongues, sucking on your lip ...

I feel you shift your weight, your leg raises and you place your foot up on the edge of the loo seat ... You move your lips to my ear and whisper, 'Touch me, touch me please ...' My hands move between us, loosening the belt of your dress so the top gapes open and I can see your breasts swelling in the lace of your bra ... I trail my lips down your neck, kissing and blowing as I go, down over your collarbone and down between your breasts, licking at your cleavage, tasting the thin film of perspiration as you start to pant quietly ... My hand drops to your thigh, feeling the stocking tops ... sliding my fingers up across your smooth skin ...

We don't have too much time, I know, so I am quick with my fingers ... My hand moves to the juncture of your thighs and I find lacy knickers, French cut ... soft, loose, flowing ... My fingers slip inside the leg, grazing your flesh and my thumb brushes against a thin strip of hair ... soft and short and narrow ... I twist my hand slightly and my fingers find you. You're wet already, I can feel the heat and the dampness between your legs ... My tongue flickers over your swollen breast and my other hand finds its way between your breasts to the clasp at the front and unclips it ... The cups fall away and I seek out your hard nipples with my tongue, licking first one, then the other ... then sucking one inside my lips and nibbling on it ...

The fingers of my other hand press against the heat between your thighs ... I feel your lips part stickily as my fingers run between them ... I slide a finger deep inside you and feel and hear you gasp as I touch those soft rippling walls ... I draw my finger out ... raise my hand to your breast and trace the sticky wet finger over and around your stiff nipple ... wetting it with your

177

cream ... my hand drops again as my mouth closes on your nipple again, tasting your pussy juices for the first time, licking and sucking them from your breast ... You taste divine, slick and wet and sticky and hot ...

I slide one, then two fingers back inside you ... God, you're hot in there ... I curl my fingers round and back towards the front of your pussy, feeling for the roughness inside which I want to find and stroke ...

I take my hands away for a second so I can fold the dress back, exposing your knickers and the damp patch at the front ... Then I release your nipple and slide to my knees in front of you and as I near your cunt I can smell you ... musky and sweet and hot ... I pull the leg of your French knickers aside and gaze at your pussy for the first time ... a thin line of hair points down to where you start to swell ... I lean forward, inhale your scent and lick slowly, softly, up your thigh and into the wet warmth of your pussy ... my nose pushes against the swell of your clitoris, throbbing softly under its hood, waiting for me to tease it out ... my tongue probes between your lips and then back to your clit ... I want to get you ready and on the point of no return quickly ... we can't have much longer on this journey ...

I flicker my tongue softly, then harder and faster over and around your clit ... my hand slides between your lips, wetting my fingers as I move my hand to cup and caress the globe of your arse, my thumb brushing, pressing against your tight little rosebud and I hear you suck air in hard as you feel me press against you ...

You're wet enough now ... but I'm not and I stand ... you look at me as I unbuckle my belt and undo the buttons of my fly ... Understanding dawns in your eyes as I move you across over the seat of the loo ... pushing down gently till you sit, wide-legged across the closed lid ... You look up at me as you work your hand inside my trousers, tugging my boxers down till my cock springs up and out at you ... You look at me, lick your lips then bob your head forward and engulf me in the hottest, wettest mouth I've ever experienced ... My eyes roll back in my head and I know I can't take too much of this ... Your lips drag slowly back up my shaft and your tongue tickles along the vein underneath ... You close your lips tightly round the tip of my cock and suck hard, flicking your tongue fast against the underside of my head and as you withdraw, sucking noisily, I see a bright red stain of lipstick round my head ...

'Come here,' I say throatily as I lift you back up again. I turn you round to face the cubicle wall and lift the back of your dress up around your waist ... My trousers fall to the floor and I move in close behind you ... my cock pressing between the cheeks of your bum ... rubbing over your asshole ... I shift myself slightly so my cock can press down between your thighs and it springs up hard against your hot pussy ... you're dripping and you're coating me with more juice ... 'Put me in you,' I mutter thickly and I feel your hand delve between us, fumbling for my prick and finding it ... you slide the head up between your lips, bumping it against your clit and then pushing it back again towards your hole ... I feel you raise yourself slightly, up on to your toes, and the tip of my cock lodges inside the opening of your pussy and as you settle down again, I feel a fiery warmth surround me as I sink deep inside you ...

Your hands braced against the wall, we settle into a rhythm, my cock sliding deep inside you, your fingers alternately strumming your clit or reaching further down to caress my balls as they swing against you as I fuck deep into you ... My hand comes up and cups a breast in

179

my palm, squeezing the nipple, releasing it ....

We're fucking harder now ... our breath coming in short gasps ... I feel you lean over towards your bag and you fumble inside it, your hand coming out, and when I hear the soft buzz, I know what you have got ...

As my cock slides in and out of you, I feel you bring your hand to where we join and I feel the vibration shudder through us both as you press the vibe to our fucking flesh ... You slide the toy up to your clit and start to pant wildly as I grind myself deep inside you ...

I slide myself inside you, then back out ... feeling your pussy clutch and clench tightly on my hardness ... the vibe pulses and throbs against your clit ... I can feel the vibration through your skin ... through your walls and into my cock inside you ...

My left hand tightens on your breast ... squeezing your flesh in my fingers ... your nipple stiff against my palm ...

My hips sway to and fro ... my cock sliding in and out of your sucking wet cunt ... your hand holding the vibe and rubbing it round and round and over your clitoris and the slippery folds around it ... I hear your breath shortening and I know you're close, feel your cunt clasping my cock and drawing me deeper and deeper inside you as I push harder into your soft giving flesh ... fucking you deep and hard and slow and soft and warm into you ... I feel your hand steal down, fumbling between your legs, groping between mine until you find what you're looking for and I feel the vibe pulsing against my balls ... your juices pour out of your pussy, down and over my balls and your fingers making us both slippery and wet and hot ...

I feel your back start to arch and your head twist round ... I lick the corner of your mouth as your breath comes in ragged gasps ... you twist your face round further and plunge your tongue into my mouth ... my left hand covers your breast, squeezing the nipple hard, restricting the blood ... numbing you slightly ... my cock pistons into you ... your hand rolls the vibe back up and over your clit and I feel my balls tighten and, deep inside you, I feel your stomach muscles clench and release, tighten into knots, your pussy walls grip firmly to my shaft and your back arches and you come ... I release your nipple and the blood rushes back in, making it tingle and throb, your clit explodes and throbs and your cunt squeezes my cock and my balls churn and spasm and I come, shooting deep inside you.. feeling your muscles milking me ... our mouths locked together, breath stopped for a moment, the heat and wet of our bodies covering us with juices and cum and sweat ... you turn the vibe off and let it drop back into your bag... I pull you closer and feel your pussy contract and release around me ...

We catch our breath, slowly, and I hear you whisper, 'I need to go,' and, not sure what you mean, I step back, my cock slipping noisily from your clasping pussy and you turn, and sink down on the loo seat and pull me back towards you again ... Your mouth opens and you engulf my sticky wet cock inside your hot sucking mouth again, licking and sucking our juices off me, tasting our cum, mingled together ...

And I hear a soft tinkle of pee hitting the bowl as you release yourself and I know what you meant now and I bend over as you suck and lick my cock clean and I reach down between your legs into the loo, and I feel the hot splash of your pee flow over my fingers as I find your clit again and swiftly, softly rub you again till you shudder once more ... coming on my fingers as you empty yourself over my hand and into the bowl ...

We catch our breath and as I wash my hands and you straighten your clothes, taking the sodden knickers off over your shoes, I look down at my cock and can still see the lipstick trace around the head ... I smile and turn to you and say, 'We really should do this more often Melinda, we really should ...'

Enter the Rainmaker
by Landon Dixon

He arrived in town on May 2, 1932. Rugby, North Dakota. Tall and lean, with curly black hair, twinkling brown eyes and a gregarious manner. His name was Russell Jameson, but he called himself the Rainmaker. And by the end of that summer, so did everybody else in Pierce County.

"Had maybe two inches of rain all last year. And not a drop so far this year," the local farm equipment dealer told him.

Not that Russell had to be told. He had eyes; parched countryside, some of the richest farmland in all of the 48 states, lay hard and cracked and barren in all directions.

He let his presence become known, chatting up the local businessmen, tipping his hat to the ladies and tousling the hair of their tow-headed children. And in doing so, *he* became aware of a presence – that of a young, blonde woman who set his pulse and his scheming mind to racing.

He was sitting in Ma's Ice Cream Parlor, enjoying a coney island and a malted milk, when she walked by the plate glass window on the plank-board sidewalk outside. Russell just about choked on his hot dog, snorted malted, as he got a good look at the girl. The land might've been

183

flatter than the devil's pancake all around, but this blonde was anything but.

Tall and slim, with long, smooth limbs bronzed by the sun, the young woman's breasts bulged out the front of her gingham dress like twin hams under tablecloth. Obscenely huge, heavy boobs that jostled and jiggled all the more provocatively as she strolled by the window, temporarily blotting out the sunshine, except in Russell's heart. Her pale blue eyes briefly met his widened-to-accommodate eyes, and then looked away.

Russell flat-out gawked, like every other man, woman, and child in the restaurant, and on the street, and in the town. The Rainmaker had seen some big tits in his day – from windblown Oklahoma to the dusty Texas panhandle up to the bone-dry river bottoms of Nebraska – but he'd never, ever seen a pair like this before. The seams of the girl's dress seemed ready to pop and unravel with every ripe, delicious double-jounce, thin cloth somehow not tearing at the twin, unfettered nipple points that jutted out from the titanic ta-ta's.

Russell's eyes bounced right along with those amazing breasts. Until the pretty blonde girl carried them out of sight, but certainly not out of mind. He turned to the wizened old sodbuster sitting at the table next to his and asked, "Say, who was that young lady just walked by?"

The wrinkled old farmer blinked, setting his wandering eyes back in their sockets. "That was Britta Lindgren," he said, wiping drooled chocolate sauce off his chin. "Biggest set of jugs outside a dairy farm."

The Rainmaker grinned, his mouth watering like he meant the clouds to do, and now the girl.

By the 4th, a group of desperate farmers and

184

townspeople had agreed to pay for Russell's services, half upfront, half on delivery. He stated that he'd already done some preliminary surveying, and determined that the best place for further pluviculture analysis and experimentation was Henk Larsen's farm just on the outskirts of town. He didn't bother mentioning that his surveying had consisted entirely of finding out that Britta Lindgren was Henk's nineteen-year-old cousin, who'd lived with the Larsens since she was five.

Henk was suspicious, downright hostile. But the other farmers convinced him, and Russell drove his silver Studebaker and rainmaking equipment out to Henk's place and went to work. He sized up the land and the sky and the wind, the few wispy clouds that ventured out into the searing heat. Striding around in Henk's arid fields and taking notes, measurements, a studious look on his handsome mug.

And when there wasn't a crowd of apprehensive men and curious kids watching his every move, he scrutinized the weather charts and almanacs, scouted out a crop duster for hire. And studied, up-close, the fine, chest-blessed form of young, blonde Britta Lindgren; whose clear blue eyes no longer looked away when they met Russell's.

"You'll really take me away from this godforsaken place – to New York City!?" breasty Britta beseeched Russell, in the back of Henk's barn. "Honest!?"

Russell smiled, flashing all twenty-eight of his natural teeth and four falsies (replacing the other originals that were scattered about various barroom floors and hay lofts across the country). He'd been spoon-feeding the heavy-titted teenager sugar-sweet tales of his adventures in the big cities, and now he gripped her brown, blondefuzzed arms and gazed into her sparkling eyes with all the sincerity he could muster.

"You bet I will, sweetheart. Why, someone with your obvious ... charms, deserves to be seen and appreciated by more than just a few hicks in the sticks." Russell licked his red lips, eyeing the twin globes almost bursting the front of the girl's white summer dress, begging to be explored. "Honey, you're too big for a place like this."

Britta clapped her hands together and squealed, her skin tingling under Russell's firm, warm grasp; Russell's eyes lost in the shivering tan depths of her cleavage. The hot sun beat down on the pair of them, no shade behind that decrepit barn except directly beneath Britta's balcony. Russell slowly moved his head forward, and touched his lips to hers, his hands sliding lower down her arms, thumbs brushing up against the swollen sides of the girl's boobs.

Britta impulsively threw her arms around Russell's neck and mashed her mouth against his, her brain dizzy with the promise of freedom, her body buzzing with the prospect of first-time release. She excitedly chewed on Russell's lips, hungrily consuming what the Rainmaker was selling.

Her awesome breastworks bounding up against his chest knocked Russell breathless for a moment. But he quickly recovered, wrapping his arms around the built babe and meeting her thrashing pink tongue with his. Her tremendous tits were hot and huge and soft against his heaving chest, and his cock flowered up in his flannels like a corn stalk after a spring shower, pressing hard and insistent into Britta's warm belly.

They were both sweating, breathing heavily, urgently kissing and frenching one another, Britta inhaling the man's musky aftershave through her nostrils, Russell the busty doll's sweet perfume, the wet perfume between her legs. He grasped her shoulders and shoved her back, breaking mouth contact, but not chest contact. He smoothly slid her dress off her shoulders and pulled it down. The gasping girl stood with her arms at her sides, as the thin cotton caressed the mountainous tops of her breasts, crested the jutting peaks, then plummeted down the breathtaking spherical descent to her waist.

Russell gaped at the sun-browned hills of paradise, mesmerized by their beauty. They were as richly tanned and smooth as the rest of the girl, attesting to her obvious irrepressibility, their bronzed nipples sprouting hard and thick as pumpkin stems from hand-spanning areolas of a slightly darker hue. Round, silk-skinned, unblemished melons that hung overripe for the picking from the slender, supple vine of Britta's body.

The Rainmaker swallowed dry, unable even to conjure up any spit in the presence of those magnificent breasts. He sucked hot air into his lungs and closed the two inches between his shaking hands and the Rushmoric boobs. Britta yelped with pleasure, Russell with delight, as he touched the warm, stretched skins, clasped and squeezed the velvety-smooth, overflowing flesh.

His sweaty hands fell short of his grasping ambition, however, because the girl's tits were just too large for one man to fully handle. But he did his best, groping the fresh, pliable meat, thumbing and then rolling the inch-long rubbery nipples, basking in the heated glory of the teenager's twin miracles of nature.

Heaving up the spilling bottoms of her jugs and locking his elbows into his sides, he bent his head down and pushed her breasts up and was just about to take a pull on a hardened nipple, when someone said, "I thought you was after water, not milk?"

Britta's mams jumped along with the rest of her body in Russell's hands. They cranked their heads sideways – to look at Grun Torsten, Henk's simple-minded farmhand. The lanky, redheaded work-shirker was peeking around the corner of the barn, staring bug-eyed at Britta's Russell-cupped udders.

Britta turned red as Grun's hair. She yanked up her dress and ran away around the opposite side of the barn. Leaving Russell embarrassingly empty-handed to explain.

On the 6th, the Rainmaker put on a real show for the locals out in a fallow field. Setting ablaze bonfires and setting off explosions – to coax the clouds. At the end of it all promising rain, soon. And that night, delivering. Just shortly after he'd stepped out of the crop duster he'd used to sprinkle the promising clouds with his 'secret chemicals'.

It started as a trickle, at midnight. By one, it was pouring. Coming down in big, fat, wet drops and soaking into the thirsty ground. Drumming on the rooftops and rattling against the windowpanes, music to people's ears. Silver in the clouded moonlight; a hundred times more valuable.

Russell reunited with Britta behind the barn. After he'd made sure the rest of the farm family and animals were bedded down for the night, the wonderful rain lulling them into pleasant dreams. He found the topsy girl standing out in the storm with her head tilted back and her arms outstretched, golden hair streaming down her back, cotton dress flush to her lush body. Her boobs heaved under the thin, saturated material, nipples nosing

188

right through.

Russell grabbed her in his arms and rained moist kisses down on her damp, slender neck, her dripping chin and wet lips, drinking in the pure, sweet dewiness of the girl. She shuddered like the thunder, and he pushed her up against the slick, weathered boards of the barn and filled his hands to overflowing with tit, urgently kneading the succulent flesh. She whimpered when he tore her soaked dress apart; moaned when he gripped her bare, brimming breasts as best he could and swam his tongue all over her shining nipples.

He licked one dripping spigot, then the other, swirling his tongue all around the engorged nipples, revelling in their rubbery taste, the pebbly texture of her rain-dappled areolas. Always working and working the thick mass of her tits.

She twisted her head from side to side against the barn, her water-washed body and breasts surging with electricity like the low-hanging sky. Then she reached down under her manhandled ledges and clawed the Rainmaker's pants open, pulled his divining rod – hot and throbbing in her hand – out of his underwear.

Russell groaned from around a mouth-filling nipple, thrilling with the feel of the girl's soft, stroking hand on his cock. He really chewed on her meaty tit-caps, ruggedly hefting her hooters. Then he slammed the mammoth mammaries together and swiped his tongue across both pointed peaks at once, rain dancing off the trembling tops of the fleshy canopies. He licked and sucked and groped for as long as he could. Until the girl's insistently tugging hand triggered a storm in his balls, steam in his dong.

He kneed her legs apart and plunged like lightning inside of her, deep into her inner wetness; bursting the dam of her desire. She cried out with all her roiling heart and soul, her breasts heaving like buoys on a churning ocean in his sweating hands. The force of his pumping hips splashed her up against the barn over and over, making her head swim, flooding her body with a liquid heat.

He was lost in a sea of lust himself, frantically fucking, fondling her, filling his salivating mouth and slippery mitts with wet-nurse nipple and wet-dream breast. His soaking, stroking cock surging with molten semen that knew only one all-out release.

They gushed their ecstasy together, bathing one another in their steaming juices. The warm rain washing over them in shimmering waves.

Henk Larsen watched from behind the tool shed, dick in one hand, axe in the other. Beady eyes burning bright in the jungle rain of the night with the lust and rage of the man who'd vowed to be Britta's first.

And when his exhausted, exhilarated cousin finally gathered her sodden dress together over her plundered treasure chest and ran for the house, he oozed around the shed and in behind Russell, using the rain as cover. He brought the axe up over his head. Then crashed its sharp, gleaming blade down onto Russell's skull. Cleaving it in two.

Henk buried the body in some brush ten feet away from the bank of the trickling creek that bordered his property. Some townsfolk wondered where the Rainmaker had gotten to. While Britta could only bitterly swallow what she was now sure were the con-man's empty promises. But the farmers didn't care – they had their rain. And more rain.

All through May and into June. By late June, the

fields were flooded, the struggling crops drowned.

It rained just about all summer long. And by early September, the normally docile rivers and creeks were dangerously swollen, filled to their banks with ugly, brown, churning waters.

Henk Larsen was crossing the short wooden bridge over the creek and onto his land the night of the 7th, the surging water making the bridge tremble. He was almost to the far bank, when it suddenly gave way upstream, earth and brush and trees sliding into the raging current in a crumbling shelf.

A wall of water welled up over the bridge and slammed into his Model T pick-up. The truck shimmied sideways in the rushing tide, the man inside gripping the wheel and watching in horror as the body of Russell Jameson slithered down the broken bank and slid into the angry water, bobbed up and rode the crest, landed with a jarring thud against the cab of Henk's pick-up.

The terrified farmer stared at the split skull gleaming ethereally in the sheet lightning, its jaw chattering with the torrent of the current, calling to Henk out of the pounding rain. He scrambled to the other side of the cab, clawed the door open, and jumped out. Right into the cold, muddy, charging, debris-choked water.

Britta attended Russell's funeral only. Along with other well-endowed women from other States who brought with them children bearing more than a passing resemblance to the man; truly attesting to his 'seeding' ability. Britta was five months along, herself.

And when they finally laid the Rainmaker to rest in the moist earth, the sun was shining. Not a cloud in the sky.

Girl Crush
by Sommer Marsden

'There isn't much I wouldn't do for you,' I said and then laughed. The laughter was nerves.

'Then just think about it. I know it's cliché but it's something I can't get out of my head,' Scott said. He pulled me close and smoothed my hair. 'We're on vacation and we're here to be wild and free. And maybe a teeny tiny bit dirty,' he snickered and then delivered a hot wet kiss to my collarbone.

'I'll think about it,' I sighed on a shiver. That one hot kiss had awakened every nerve in my body.

'Dinner?'

'Dinner,' I agreed and followed him out.

The dining room was gorgeous. The hotel had gone all out to make it magical and elegant and sexy all at the same time. Long, white tablecloths on the small, intimate tables. Candlelight. Low lighting from the crystal chandeliers. We had been at the Palms for two nights and every night I looked forward to dinner. The setting alone was erotic.

'My name is Callie and I'll be your server tonight,' the waitress said.

'Hi, we had you the night before last,' I said, accepting the menu.

Callie nodded, her long, dark hair hiding her face for just a moment, and she smiled. 'I remember. How are you? Enjoying your stay?'

When I glanced up, her eyes were fixed on the low-cut V of my red dress. She caught me looking and her pale cheeks were instantly stained with rosy pink. Scott's big warm hand crept up my thigh, hidden from view by the tablecloth. Had he planned this?

'Lovely,' I said, my voice a little high. *She* was really lovely. Callie. Tall and slender with all that long, dark hair. 'Thank you.'

Still blushing, she nodded and shared a glance with my husband. 'Sir, what can I get you to drink?' she asked in a small voice.

'Whatever's on draft,' Scott said. 'What about you, Paige?'

'A glass of Merlot,' I said, looking not at him but directly at Callie.

She dipped her head and hid behind that hair again. 'Yes, ma'am. I'll be right back with your drinks.' She scampered off like a puppy.

'What have you done?' I hissed, swatting Scott's big arm. 'Did you set me up?'

He laughed. It wasn't a malicious laugh but the kind of laugh that comes from being married for a very long time. 'All I did was request to be seated in her section. She has a girl crush on you.' He put his arm around my shoulder and stroked by bare skin. I sighed and allowed myself to be pulled close.

'What the hell is a girl crush?'

My husband leaned in and whispered right in my ear. His hot breath ignited all the little nerve endings in my face. My pulse throbbed and my nipples grew tight under the bodice of my dress.

'When a younger girl has a crush on an older woman. Well, in this case. Can be any time. High school, work place, whatever. Usually she looks up to the other woman. Wants to be like her or look like her or learn from her. Remember the article I read? I tried to read some to you.'

'You're always trying to read things to me. Sometimes I just ...'

'Tune me out?' he whispered and subtly let his hand drop from my shoulder to my breast. One quick pinch of my nipple, so fast it was like a magic trick, and my cunt flooded in my expensive silk panties.

'Mmm-hmmm,' I moaned.

'Bad girl. You should know better. I only read you things that are pertinent.'

Callie returned with our drinks. Her cheeks were still flushed and she continued to hide behind the sleek curtain of dark, chocolate hair. Her eyes flashed to me, skittered over me and then darted away. She nearly toppled Scott's beer on the table. 'Sorry, sorry,' she murmured, her voice sweet and low, 'I'm all thumbs tonight.'

'It's OK,' I said, touching her hand gently. I suddenly felt very powerful. Powerful and sexy. The fact that Scott's hand had started snaking up my inner thigh under the table didn't help matters. I fought the urge to squirm in my seat. She sucked in a breath and stared at my hand. My eyes sought and found the hard nubs of her nipples behind her plain white blouse. I took my hand away and handed her the menus. 'We'll both have the steak special.'

She nodded and then practically bolted from our table. Scott's blunt finger wormed under my panties and slid straight into my wet, moist heat. 'Wetter than wet,' he snickered in my ear. 'Are you still considering it?'

I slouched just a touch in the booth so that his finger slid deep into my cunt. He quickly added a second finger and I had to control my breathing. 'No.'

Scott hooked his fingers inside of me. Nearly inaudible wet sounds emanated from under the elegant table. He probed my G-spot expertly until I gave into the quick but intense orgasm he provoked.

'No?' he smiled and then subtly stuck his fingers in his mouth and licked them clean.

Little white-hot echoes sounded inside of me at the sight. My pussy flickered and twitched, wanting more of what it had just been given. 'No. I've decided. Find out what time her shift ends.'

'Will do,' he said with a small, victorious smile.

I wasn't nervous. Why wasn't I nervous? I should be, shouldn't I?

Scott wasn't nervous either. He sat on the hotel bed and watched me. Watched me touch up my make-up. Watched me smooth my short blonde hair. Watched me straighten my dress and wash my hands and spritz a little perfume on my pulse points. He watched it all with a small, secret smile. And when my gaze met his in the mirror, I smiled too.

'She knows, right?' I asked again. I wasn't nervous but I was concerned. 'She knows why I invited her up.'

Scott gave me another patient nod. 'Judging by the way she flushed that lovely raspberry color and how hard her little nipples got ... *again* ... I'd say, yes, she knows. And if she doesn't and she wants to leave, then she can.'

'Right.' I heard the hesitant tapping on the door and my stomach bottomed out.

'She's here,' Scott said, and I could hear the excitement in his voice. This had been his fantasy for years. A tried-and-true fantasy of many men. His wife with another woman.

I found that suddenly it was my fantasy, too. Him watching me. Me and the lovely Callie.

She looked almost startled when I opened the door. As if she hadn't expected us to actually be here. 'Come on in,' I said, taking pains to keep my voice low. I didn't want to scare her.

She stood in the centre of our luxurious hotel room looking terrified but aroused. Her brown eyes were wide, the pupils dilated, her breathing rapid. For all intents and purposes, she looked as if she might run or have an orgasm at any moment.

'Can I get you a drink?' I offered. 'You seem really scared. Are you scared?'

She shook her head no and then let her eyes take me in. Her gaze levelled me from the tip of my head to the toe cleavage peaking out of my pumps. She surprised me by speaking. Loudly. 'Can we do this? I know why you asked me here. I knew the moment you touched my arm. And I am nervous but I really want this and I'd like to start.'

I heard Scott's soft laughter from the corner.

'Of course we can,' I said and began unbuttoning her blouse. She reached through my arms and untied the knot at the base of my neck. The halter of my red dress fell away, leaving my breasts bare, nipples eager.

'Oh my,' she said and then she dipped her head just as I freed the last button and she sucked my nipple into her mouth. Her tiny pink mouth.

A rush of heat shot through me. From breast to cunt. Belly to scalp. How different the feel of her delicate feminine mouth was from Scott's. More gentle. Wetter if possible. Reverent.

Her small hands roamed over the skirt of my dress, caressed my waist, and I tackled the button of her black slacks. Now I wanted her bare. I wanted to see her small breasts, the hollow of her belly button, what was nestled between her thighs. Trimmed? Bare? Shaved? Wild? I couldn't wait to find out.

My voice was more authoritative than normal. 'Step out,' I commanded as I shoved her jeans down along with her panties. I had only caught a flash of red, and beyond the colour, I had no idea what they looked like. I didn't care.

She stepped out but her hands never left me for more than a second. It was as if she were memorising me with her hands. She was smooth and bare and creamy. I glanced quickly at Scott. The fly of his trousers was tented, the small smile still on his lips. He stroked the bulge under his fly with those big hands. I felt another hot rush of fluid slide down my inner thighs.

I ditched her clothes and her bra and then shimmied out of the rest of my dress. Before I could take off my silk panties, Callie had dropped to her knees and buried her face in the sodden material that shielded my cunt. The intensity of seeing another woman face first in my crotch was overwhelming. I plunged my hands into her soft hair and felt her hot breath heat the silk.

I heard Scott's zipper in the near silence.

She licked her way around the border of my panties and my knees felt unstable. I waited patiently as she explored. Her tiny nose nuzzled my belly as she traced the covered seam of my sex with her kitten pink tongue. I felt like I would come already.

I shoved the thong down and widened my stance.

'Would you like to do it for real?' I asked softly.

She didn't even answer but rubbed the tip of her tongue over my already swollen clit as if she were taking a tiny sample taste. Very delicate and tentative but eager. My pulse slammed in my throat and chest and clit. My body thumping with each beat of my heart. I brushed her hair back so I could watch her. Her slender throat working, her eyes closed, her tongue probing and pushing and licking at me. I was fiercely wet and very hungry to see what she tasted like. Curiosity had turned to full-fledged desire.

'Back up,' I sighed, and she did but her large brown eyes looked confused. 'It's OK,' I smiled. 'Let's go over there.'

The blush returned, turning her normally creamy complexion ruddy. She dropped her eyes but nodded. I took her hand, wanting her to be comfortable, and led her to the bed.

I lay on my back and motioned her over me. I had deliberately lain sideways across the bed for Scott. This way he could see us both. See her mouth and tongue on me and mine on her. I heard the secretive wet sounds of his spit-dampened fist pumping his cock. My pussy twitched at the sound. Ready. I was ready.

When her cunt was over my face I could see how wet she was. Swollen and rosy and dilated. I did it all at once. Plunged my tongue in between her wet lips to find the tiny pink nub of her clit. Thrust two fingers into her blossoming pussy. She sighed against my own pussy and the vibration rocketed through me.

She tasted sweet and slightly musky. She tasted exotic and new. I worked my fingers into her moist heat, licked at her, drank her. Each time I licked her pussy

198

clean a fresh wave of her moisture coated my face and my chin. My lips tingled with the feel of her.

Scott groaned in the corner. I groaned on the bed as her slender fingers pushed into me. Explored me. Her tongue never stopped. Hot and fast, reminding me of the way tiny silverfish move in the ocean. Graceful and darting. Fast and intentional.

I suckled her clit and nibbled and her pussy clenched around my fingers, giving little warning signs of orgasm. I glanced at my husband as his fist pumped faster over his purplish cock. His face was divine. Intent and aroused and happy. And he was very close. Fifteen years of marriage earns you the knowledge. From the way his lips were parted and his eyes half closed, he was about to shoot and I wanted to go with him.

I played ring around the rosie with her beautiful pussy. Licking everywhere but where she wanted me until my fingers were trapped in her tight wet heat. Then I focused on her clit until she squirmed over me. Scott shifted, his fist a blur. I bucked myself against Callie's mouth and she started to finger-fuck me in earnest. I hooked my fingers inside of her and felt the swollen, suede-soft G-spot. I pushed it, stroked it and sucked her clit into my mouth.

She let loose over me. Her juices coating my face, her eager little tongue lapping at me even as she cried out. And over I went. I let her soft tongue and long fingers tip me over just as I saw my husband come. A freshet of semen shot from his fist and I rode wave after wave of pleasure.

Callie collapsed against me, twitching and cooing from time to time. I felt my breathing slow, my orgasm fade.

No one moved. Scott stared at me. His eyes barely

took in our beautiful guest. It was me he was watching.

'I have to go,' Callie said softly. Her gaze lingered on my body for just a moment, and when she smiled she looked more certain of herself. 'I have to pick up my son from the sitter.'

I rose and kissed her softly on the lips. Her tongue was a searing heat in my mouth for a moment and then she turned to get dressed.

'We're here for two more nights,' I said. I handed her the blouse. 'Do you work tomorrow?'

'Yes, I do. Would you like me to come back?'

I didn't even glance at Scott.

'I would. If you want to.'

She buttoned her blouse and grinned. 'I'll be back. I'm sure I'll see you in the dining room first.' Then she touched my arm and kissed me again. 'You're so pretty.'

I couldn't help but laugh. 'And so are you.'

I didn't get dressed even after she left. I sat in Scott's lap and noticed he was hard again. I kissed him deeply and sighed, 'See what she tastes like?'

'Delicious.'

'Mmmm-hmmm.'

'So how do you feel about my fantasy now?'

'I think it's *my* fantasy at this point. And next time you read me something, I will definitely pay attention.'

More great books from Xcite...

Naughty Spanking One
Twenty bottom-tingling stories to make your buttocks blush!
9781906125837 £7.99

The True Confessions of a London Spank Daddy
Memoir by Peter Jones
9781906373320 £7.99

Girl Fun One
Lesbian anthology edited by Miranda Forbes
9781906373672 £7.99

The Education of Victoria
Adventures in a Victorian finishing school
9781906373696 £7.99

Ultimate Curves
Erotic short stories edited by Miranda Forbes
9781906373788 Aug 09 £7.99

Naughty! The Xcite Guide to Sexy Fun
How To book exploring edgy, kinky sex
9781906373863 Oct 09 £9.99

For more information and great offers
please visit
www.xcitebooks.com